"The study of folksingers and their songs is above all a quest for authenticity—an idea fiercely debated yet rarely defined. Into this melee of currents comes Henry Adam Svec's flagship, in the form of a book that wants to find the truth as much as anyone, but in a mirrored hall of connected folk personas that are all real in their own way: who we are, who we think we are, and who we want or need to be. It is deeply personal as much as it is a rich performance—like the best folk songs are."

— KATE BEATON, AUTHOR OF *HARK! A VAGRANT*

"A book that twangs and spirals—*sui generis* in the history of Canadian literature. Svec exhibits the acumen of Marshall McLuhan, the heart of Rita MacNeil, and the meticulous truthfulness of Farley Mowat."

— SEAN MICHAELS, SCOTIABANK GILLER PRIZE WINNER AND
AUTHOR OF *THE WAGERS*

"Fact and fiction blend and blur throughout the pages of the life of this intrepid folksong collector. What do seventies football players, itinerant rock musicians, bureaucratic academics, and artificial intelligence all have in common? Possibly nothing, but this book—with trenchant wit and performative verve—connects these and many other dots, at the same time ensuring you'll completely enjoy the ride. Perhaps we are all folklorists in the end, searching for an authenticity that can take us out of our comfort zones, replacing them with songs we didn't know we needed but now will always want to sing. Henry Adam Svec shows us how."

— JACOB WREN, AUTHOR OF *AUTHENTICITY IS A FEELING*

LIFE IS LIKE CANADIAN FOOTBALL AND OTHER AUTHENTIC FOLK SONGS

HENRY ADAM SVEC

Invisible Publishing
Halifax & Prince Edward County

Library and Archives Canada Cataloguing in Publication

Title: Life is like Canadian football and other authentic folk songs / Henry Adam Svec.

Names: Svec, Henry Adam, author.

Identifiers: Canadiana (print) 20210168773 | Canadiana (ebook) 2021016896X | ISBN 9781988784700 (softcover) ISBN 9781988784786 (HTML)

Classification: LCC PS8637.V43 L54 2021 | DDC C813/.6—dc23

Edited by Leigh Nash
Cover and interior design by Megan Fildes | Typeset in Laurentian
With thanks to type designer Rod McDonald

Printed and bound in Canada

Invisible Publishing | Halifax & Prince Edward County
www.invisiblepublishing.com

Published with the generous assistance of the Canada Council for the Arts, the Ontario Arts Council, and the Government of Canada.

 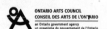 

Often does the memory of former times come, like the evening sun, on my soul.

—Ossian

You never know what you're going to get as a receiver.

—Darren Flutie

Attach yourself to what you feel to be true. Begin there.

—The Invisible Committee

INTRODUCTION

A LONG TIME AGO

To partake in the collection of folk song is to partake in the communication of the real. My progenitors and peers and opponents alike have been building this tradition for millennia now—a generations-spanning assignment of attending and recording. For this reason, the inaugural inductees into folk song collection's hall of fame must not be Johann Gottfried Herder or the Brothers Grimm, but the first literary writers *tout court*, those mediums who conjured *The Epic of Gilgamesh* and *The Iliad* out of the fog of oral conveyance and down into the relative fixity of inscription.[1]

However, the most significant starting place for the author of the present book is with James Macpherson, the Scottish man of letters who, in the mid-eighteenth century, discovered the first "legitimate" scribblings by the medieval bard called Ossian.[2] At the crest of an allegedly light-filled epoch, where reason and rationality were silently lauded, these newly unveiled treasures commanded readers back to the warm bosoms, and bowels, of being.[3] Of course, Ossian himself should also receive credit. Nonetheless, the remnant fragments of Ossian's poetry might never have been located, and reanimated in the bustling marketplaces of print, if not for Macpherson pluck-

---

1   Anonymous, *The Epic of Gilgamesh*, trans. Nancy K. Sanders (Hardmondsworth, UK: Penguin, 1972); Homer, *The Iliad*, trans. E. V. Rieu (London, UK: Penguin, 2003).

2   James Macpherson, *The Poems of Ossian Translated by James Macpherson* (London, UK: Strahan and T. Cadell, 1796).

3   See Dafydd Moore, *Enlightenment and Romance in James Macpherson's The Poems of Ossian: Myth, Genre and Cultural Change* (New York: Routledge, 2017); Celestina Savonius-Wroth, "Bardic Ministers: Scotland's Gaelic-Speaking Clergy in the Ossian Controversy," *Eighteenth-Century Studies* 52, no. 2 (2019): 225–243.

ing the poems out of the back of a dilapidated fireplace. First published more than a century before Thomas Alva Edison invented his sound-recording machine, Ossian's voice nevertheless echoed into the *aurem interiorem* of significant historical actors like Thomas Jefferson, Johann Wolfgang von Goethe, and Napoléon Bonaparte.[4] Consider the possibility: each of these prime movers, upon first reading Ossian's words, delivered by way of Macpherson and then packaged into a literary commodity for mass consumption, had never been so moved.

In fact, on the eve of his vanquishment of the Russians and Austrians at Austerlitz, Napoléon famously set down his leather-bound volume and wept.[5] The words on the page must have appeared as salve to the finally reposing tactician, snow falling across Moravia at dusk, calming and carrying the Emperor back through the deep recesses of time. One can hear the silence arriving, the battle cries faltering, and the slow swelling—the pure gushing—of primordial sonorousness. Such a transcendent aesthetic experience could only have strengthened Napoléon's constitution, enabling him to push further and harder into the wider world.

Which leads to my preliminary question: What would our modern maps look like, or sound like, if indeed they could look or sound like anything at all, if not for the blood and guts of the folklorists?

LET'S GO A-HUNTIN'

In the United States, Francis James Child made his contribution by chasing down snippets of medieval balladry, songs that we now call the Child Ballads in honour of their

---

4   On Ossian's translation into the American context, see Jack McLaughlin, "Jefferson, Poe, and Ossian," *Eighteenth-Century Studies* 26, no. 4 (1993): 627-34.

5   Presumably Napoléon was working with the French edition. See *Ossian, fils de Fingal, barde du troisième siècle: Poésies Galliques traduites sur l'anglais de M. Macpherson*, 2 Vols (Paris: 1777).

conduit.[6] Child was a professor of English literature at Harvard University, so it is logical that his primary sources would remain strictly textual.[7] Later, at the turn of the twentieth century, John A. Lomax changed the rules of the game by tracking down cowboys singing their tunes in the flesh.[8] Traipsing across America's buttes and plains, publishing calls in local periodicals, Lomax got his hands dirty, and also, presumably, his ears. We would have neither "My Darling Clementine" nor "Home on the Range" without Lomax's pioneering fieldwork.

Meanwhile, Canadian folk song collection begins roughly in the second quarter of the twentieth century, when adventurers including Helen Creighton, Marius Barbeau, and Maud Karpeles scoured the hinterlands of the Maritime provinces, Quebec, and Newfoundland, intent on registering the pastoral produce they believed was threatened by technology and mass media, among other contaminating influences.[9] They were after "organic" as opposed to "artificial" musical materials.[10] Subsequent waves of collection and analysis have lent

---

6   Francis James Child, *The English and Scottish Popular Ballads, Volumes 1-10* (Boston, MA: Houghton, Mifflin & Co., 1882-1898).

7   On the complexities of Child's understanding of ballad transmission and aesthetics, see Michael J. Bell, "'No Borders to the Ballad Maker's Art': Francis James Child and the Politics of the People," *Western Folklore* 47, no. 4 (1988): 285–307.

8   Benjamin Filene, *Romancing the Folk: Public Memory and American Roots Music* (Chapel Hill, NC: University of North Carolina Press, 2000).

9   As the historian Ian McKay has argued, focusing in particular on Creighton's legacy, song collection in Atlantic Canada can be understood as an anti-modernist and ideological project, the function of which has been to obscure the complex and dynamic conflicts within capitalistic modernity. Ian McKay, *The Quest of the Folk: Antimodernism and Cultural Selection in Twentieth-Century Nova Scotia* (Montreal, QC: McGill-Queen's University Press, 1994). For similarly critical approaches to the legacy of Barbeau, see also Andrew Nurse, Gordon Ernest Smith, and Lynda Jessup, eds., *Around and About Marius Barbeau: Modelling Twentieth-Century Culture* (Gatineau, QC: Canadian Museum of Civilization, 2008).

10   John Storey, *Inventing Popular Culture* (Malden, MA: Blackwell Publishing, 2003).

breadth to an ever-expanding archive; anthologies have been made of the folk songs of Saskatchewan, New Brunswick, and Ontario, among others.[11]

Indeed, the industry of folk song collection runs like a superabundant mineral mine, the jewels ready to withstand inexhaustible processes of extraction, assemblage, and sale. Ancient and medieval folk performers were required to choose selections in order to perform, given the physical limitations of human speech and time.[12] Modern gatherers and preservers of the folk have, for the most part, avoided this curatorial approach. Thus the modern reader of the printed folk song text is in possession of an often-encyclopedic totality of possible combinations of folkloristic information, in addition to various historical and sociological data through which said information can be situated and interpreted.[13] Some of the masterpieces in this tradition weigh over ten kilograms per volume.

I am not here to criticize. There are benefits to the mode of presentation described above, just as there are benefits to the purchase of bushels of D-grade gemstones, if one's purpose is to build a mound of gemstones. From another angle, however, one can begin to glimpse ways in which the author of the exemplary modern folk song text has tended to display tunes and tales as desiccated specimens on a table, to group their data into allegedly discrete categories, and to present their findings as the contents of a static reservoir. This is unfortunate because the object of study—folk song—is neither dry, nor categorizable, nor static. The

---

11 Barbara Cass-Beggs, *Folk Songs of Saskatchewan* (New York, NY: Folkways Records, 1963); Edith Fowke, *Lumbering Songs from the Northern Woods* (Austin, TX: University of Austin Press for the American Folklore Society, 1970); Edward D. Ives, *Folk Songs of New Brunswick* (Fredericton, NB: Goose Lane Editions, 1989).

12 Albert Bates Lord, *The Singer of Tales* (New York, NY: Athaneum, 1960).

13 Elizabeth L. Eisenstein, *The Printing Press as an Agent of Change: Communications and Cultural Transformations in Early Modern Europe* (New York: Cambridge University Press, 1979).

object of study is in fact a muddy and mobile target that must be followed in real time.

Furthermore, the author of the exemplary modern folk song text has rarely reckoned with the sources and structures of their own biases. *Why have I chosen the songs I have chosen? Why have I chosen these songs and not others? Who am I?* These questions have gone unasked and unanswered. The intermediaries engaged in folk song collection have therefore rarely achieved the authenticity and sincerity they have so often demanded of their subjects, of their folk.[14]

AS I ROVED OUT

I claim that an existential account of folk song, Canadian or otherwise, has yet to be written. Such a text would of course need to include songs themselves; additional requirements are the texture and fabric of the nets used to corral and capture each and every last gathered morsel. I am not alluding only to technology and scholarly methodology, but additionally to the taste and disposition, and thus the life, of the collector.

For although we still have Macpherson's treasures, we do not have—and will never have—a rigorous account of his experience of finding Ossian's mouldy poems. And although we have collections of countless stories and songs thanks to Creighton and Barbeau and Karpeles, we do not yet have— and will never have—a robust description of the fun they had in the thrill of the hunt, the dark desires that propelled their

---

14 Both authenticity and sincerity are significant within the field of Canadian folk song collection, though in different measures and applications. According to Lionel Trilling's account, sincerity has a social valence, whereas authenticity is understood as a non-instrumental end in itself. Lionel Trilling, *Sincerity and Authenticity* (Cambridge, MA: Harvard University Press, 1971). We might then say that Canadian folk song collectors have until now aspired toward *sincerity* in their professional identities and personas while also aspiring, as collectors, to capture the *authentic* being of the folk. This is not to say, however, that Canadian folk song collectors have tended to be very self-aware regarding these aspirations.

expeditions, or the rich resentments that fueled their drive toward discovery.[15] In other words, we have not yet *listened* to the folk in its copious totality, which includes "the folk" per se and the songs thereof, but also the disciplines and inter-mediaries (such as Creighton, Barbeau, and Karpeles—and me) through which "the folk" as a concept has been written and rewritten again, whether with dark ink, magnetic tape, electronic circuitry, or oral performance.[16] Having collected folk songs for the past decade or so, at the time of this writing, I would therefore like to take the opportunity that so many of my predecessors and contemporaries have neglected to take.

According to Werner Heisenberg's uncertainty principle, to gaze at an experiment is to fundamentally alter the structure of the observed reality.[17] Should not the same be said of folk-

---

15 Of course, I am not the first folk song collector to write an autobiographical or even a semi-autobiographical text. Helen Creighton chronologically recount-ed her development as folk song collector and person in her book *A Life in Folklore*, and Alan Lomax reflected on his own experiences throughout his ample oeuvre, including his celebrated publication *The Land Where the Blues Began*. Helen Creighton, *Helen Creighton: A Life in Folklore* (Toronto, ON: McGraw-Hill Ryerson, 1975); Alan Lomax, *The Land Where the Blues Began* (New York, NY: Pantheon Books, 1993). However, the bulk of this writing has been clearly plagued by bad-faith repression and obscene self-promotionalism, which we must seek to juke, or dodge, in a Livingstonian fashion.

16 The notion that concepts are both produced and productive is generally attrib-uted to the work of Michel Foucault. See, for example, Michel Foucault, *The Order of Things: An Archeology of the Human* Sciences (New York, NY: Pantheon, 1971). The idea that concepts are produced and productive—but in ways owing to the media technologies through which those concepts have been articulated—is often attributed to German literature scholar Friedrich Kittler. See Friedrich Kit-tler, *Gramophone, Film, Typewriter*, trans. Geoffrey Winthrop-Young and Michael Wutz (Stanford, CA: Stanford University Press, 1999). However, I must also acknowledge here Regina Bendix's institutional, if not existential, history of the discipline of folklore, which similarly approaches the concept of the folk as a constructed category. Regina Bendix, *In Search of Authenticity: The Formation of Folklore Studies* (Madison, WI: The University of Wisconsin Press, 1997). And do not forget Rosemary Lévy Zumwalt, *American Folklore Scholarship: A Dialogue of Dissent* (Bloomington, IN: Indiana University Press, 1988). As you can see, research on folk song is nearly as collaborative and intertextual as the folk itself.

17 Werner Heisenberg, *The Physical Principles of the Quantum Theory*, trans. Karl Eckart and Frank C. Hoyt (Chicago, IL: University of Chicago Press, 1930).

loristic technique? Should not the acts of looking, longing, and capturing thus be included—as primary sources—alongside any folkloristic transmission? The *Oxford English Dictionary* claims that folk song is defined as "song[s] originating from the common people; also, […] modern imitation[s] of such […] song[s]." But what does it mean to originate and to imitate? How does one know when and in what context to, for example, originate rather than imitate? Or vice versa? My hunch is that a rigorous exploration of these terms has the potential not only to refine but, in fact, to explode and thereafter regenerate the very concept of authentic folk song.[18] Accordingly, you can ponder as Molotov cocktail—but also as fertilizer—the blunt fact of the pages that follow, across which the art of the folk song collector is conceived as nothing more, and nothing less, than the art of the folksinger.[19] The parasite must become a host.[20]

To be clear, the purpose of the present volume is therefore to collect and to communicate, in a single text, the most significant folk songs that I myself have yet brought to light. At the time of writing, I have been performing (often at a financial loss) and teaching the songs collected here for nearly a decade, but I have not yet left behind the detailed diagram, setting out the development of my techniques of song collecting, that I believe is warranted. I want to inscribe—to carve out that which I have done. Desiring more than to offer a

---

18   Cf. Jacques Derrida, *Of Grammatology*, trans. Gayatri Chakravorty Spivak (Baltimore, MD: Johns Hopkins University Press, 1997).

19   Hence, for my future folkloristic interpreters, the classical structuralist analyses common in the field might be applied to either the poetry collected in the present text or the prose. Try, for example, Northrop Frye, *Anatomy of Criticism: Four Essays* (Princeton, NJ: Princeton University Press, 1957); Vladimir Propp, *Morphology of the Folk Tale*, trans. Laurence Scott (Austin, TX: University of Austin Press, 1968); Stith Thompson, *Motif-Index of Folk-Literature: A Classification of Narrative Elements in Folktales, Ballads, Myths, Fables, Mediaeval Romances, Exempla, Fabliaux, Jest-Books, and Local Legends* (Bloomington, IN: Indiana University Press, 1955–1958).

20   Michel Serres, *The Parasite*, trans. Lawrence R. Schehr (Minneapolis, MN: University of Minnesota Press, 2007).

static compendium organized by theme or region or "motif,"
I additionally aim to dramatize the folklorist's development
as such.[21] Therefore, I have collected here only those particular songs that have contributed to public apperception of folk
song in the twenty-first century, in which I have played a role.

The main body of the present volume follows a basic
chronological order. In "Songs of the Basement," I offer a
selection of Staunton R. Livington's CFL Sessions, a series of
field recordings conducted in the 1970s, which I discovered
in the basement of a hegemonic Canadian cultural apparatus
in 2008—the fortuitous act that nudged me onto my present
path. With "Songs of the Field," I share a sampling of songs
field recorded by me within the contingent and arbitrary bor-
derlines of Canada. And "Songs of the Cloud" presents the
most interesting compositions generated by the artificially
intelligent folk song database that I co-authored in 2013 while
in Dawson City, Yukon. Interspersed throughout these chap-
ters is an episodically structured *Volkskunderoman*, across
which the development of my philosophy of song collection,
and the development of my self, are chronicled.[22] Lastly, beefy
acknowledgment and bibliographic sections house complete

---

21   For the sake of sharp contrast, consider the school of folkloristic research
inspired by Russian formalism and structuralism, which seeks to reduce Folk
Poetry to a mechanistic structure across which oppositions and conflicts are
played out and resolved. See, for example, Vladimir Propp, *Morphology of the
Folktale* (1968; Austin: University of Texas Press, 1984); and Stith Thompson,
The Folk Tale (1946; Berkeley, CA: University of California Press, 1977).

22   *Volkskunderoman* is a neologism coined, as far as I am aware, by me in this
very sentence. It elegantly combines the German *Künstlerroman*—or novel
of artistic development—with the famously German term for the folk, *Volk*.
Denotatively, the word clearly conveys the form of the present text. The Germanic connotations, however, are strictly to be understood as ironical, given
the chasmic distance between the Livingstonian conception of the folk, which
is high-modernist, and that found in the original Germanic sources, which
is romantic. For discussion of the *Künstlerroman* in the context of Canadian
narrative communication, see Sian Harris, "The Canadian Künstlerroman:
The Creative Protagonist in LM Montgomery, Alice Munro and Margaret Laurence," PhD dissertation, Newcastle University, 2009.

information regarding the vast sources, both living and dead, consulted in the production of this book.

It is of course possible to begin at the beginning. However, more adventurous readers may wish to chart a different path through the present text by starting with the references and working backwards.[23] One might wish—including, perhaps, the career-minded folklorists I know—to read the songs first. This decision will be of no consequence, however, because, as the folk itself knows intuitively, time is not necessarily chronological; it is possible to experience existence as an eternal repetition of a single event, like the refrain of a folk song—or like a touchdown.[24]

Ours are terrifying yet promising times; opportunities abound.[25] I fear that my life's work will now be easy prey for cultural industries—that these songs will be commodified as a bound, bourgeois shelf decoration, the base reality of so many "folk" anthologies, and subsequently as episodic television series, T-shirts, and echoic VR experiences.[26] Who knows the limits of the logic of capital? But I also hope that the song, the collector, the medium, and the addressee will

---

23 I myself prefer to begin any book with the bibliographical sections. In my view, one wants to peruse, virtually, the libraries and archives in which the author has spent their time before joining their text on its unspooling journey. Furthermore, it is possible to decide, before even finishing the bibliography, whether or not the author is a responsible researcher. And in some fascinating examples, the bibliography is the central text, thereby calling into question the distinction. See, for example, Peter Meyer Filardo, "United States Communist History Bibliography 2018," *American Communist History* 18, no. 1-2 (2019): 97–168.

24 The concept of recurrence has on occasion assuaged the present author's anxieties, as he has confronted the infinity of sensations, experiences, events, and interpretations that might have made it into the present text, required in the end to boil everything down into a single, advancing line. A task which has seemed all but impossible in my weakest hours. See Mirceau Eliade, *The Myth of the Eternal Return* (Princeton, NJ: Princeton University Press, 1905).

25 Donna Haraway, *Staying with the Trouble: Making Kin in the Chthulucene* (Durham, NC: Duke University Press, 2016).

26 See Max Horkheimer and Theodor W. Adorno, *The Dialectic of Enlightenment* (Stanford, CA: Stanford University Press, 2002).

be codirected toward purposeful triumph, by way of struggle and resolution.

Alas, much must be left to you, dear reader, or receiver, for I am not a psychologist, or even a librarian. Within the current communicative context, I am only a humble scribe who modestly hopes that this volume's motley mix of songs, scholarship, and story will provoke my opponents within the so-called sanctioned bastions of folk song collection. Yet, my greatest desire for the present text is that it will circulate beyond all official gates and walls, to inspire the next generation of authentic folk song collectors, and, therefore, folksingers. Will you be among them?

part one

SONGS OF THE BASEMENT

WHEN THE STARS BEGIN TO FALL

An attitude exists—which can be more precisely termed an ideology, for it is both arbitrary and partisan—under the spell of which one's ambitions appear subject to the sovereignty of exterior actants.[1] Through this lens the world becomes a transportive contraption, like a carnival ride or Dictaphone; one simply flicks the switch and receives what comes. *Will I be called upon to play in the big game? Will the quarterback throw me the long bomb? Will hidden Canadian cultural treasures finally disclose themselves? Will the revolution be permitted?* Under the spell of this kind of questioning, there is little to do but wait and see.

Where does this ideology come from? How does it function?[2] On one hand, fate has the capacity to console in times of crisis. For example, when Canadian cultural treasures do not ultimately reveal themselves to a suchlike treasure hunter, the concept of inevitability operates as ointment, or laudanum, for the accompanying feelings of failure. This is a defense mechanism. Rather than attributing loss to individual weaknesses, or to the exploitative essence of capitalism, the claim can be made that it was just not in the cards, an excuse equally available to folklorists, fullbacks, and fascistic Silicon Valley entrepreneurs.

On the other hand, the concept of fate can amplify the ego in times of plenty. When a player scores the winning touch-

---

1   Karl Marx and Friedrich Engels, *The German Ideology* (New York, NY: International Publishers, 1947).

2   For a precise and technical analyses of ideology and its functioning, see Louis Althusser, *Lenin and Philosophy, and other Essays*, trans. Ben Brewster (London, UK: New Left Books, 1971). See also Judith Butler, *Gender Trouble: Feminism and the Subversion of Identity* (New York, NY: Routledge, 1999); Stuart Hall, "Signification, Representation, Ideology: Althusser and the Post-Structuralist Debates," *Critical Studies in Media Communication* 2, no. 2 (1985): 91-114; Slavoj Žižek, *The Sublime Object of Ideology* (New York, NY: Verso, 1989).

down in the big game, for instance, it might feel as though the preceding movements of their own hands and limbs were long ago scrawled down by some sagacious scribe, across some lustrous surface. "It is written, and so it shall be, and so I have done," the champion might cry while spiking the ball into the end zone's turf, or playfully wiggling their bum. Victory on any field must be attributed to the complex inter-penetration of economic and political machinations—to the (contingent) structuring processes of privilege, oppression, and exploitation combined with the (chaotic) responses of individual players.[3] I do not have room to explain here in further detail the complexities of historical metamorphosis.[4] However, embracing the notion that *what must exist will exist* is less conceptually difficult. Thus, mottoes in this fashion conceptually lubricate (i.e., enable) action in games, markets, wars, and bedrooms alike.

Was I destined to discover the CFL Sessions? More than one bumbling CBC journalist has asked. It is true that there had been only a vague awareness, on my part, of Staunton R. Livingston's output when I began my internship at Library and Archives Canada in the spring of 2008. Livingston was a ghost, a cipher, spoken about in reverential whispers near water coolers in campus/community radio stations, yet he left few clear documentary traces. Furthermore, rather than having unearthed Livingston's tapes in the virile acts of rum-maging or foraging, the unmarked box carrying the Sessions fell, in fact, directly upon my head while I was shortcutting through the processing shelves one rainy morning on my way

---

3   Karl Marx, *The Eighteenth Brumaire of Louis Bonaparte* (New York, NY: Interna-tional Publishers, 1964).

4   See Erin Morton, *For Folk's Sake: Art and Economy in Twentieth-Century Nova Scotia*, (Montreal, QC: McGill-Queen's University Press, 2016); Karl Polanyi, *The Great Transformation: The Political and Economic Origins of Our Time*, 2nd Edition (Boston, MA: Beacon Press, 2001); or Raymond Williams, *Television: Technology and Cultural Form* (London: Routledge, 2003).

to the toilet.[5] These details do lead credence to the destiny narrative, toward which we can imagine the average CBC broadcaster gravitating in the production of a characteristically spectacular exposé.[6]

I know I am not preordained to sustain the weight of a forgotten generation of cultural producers. My deeds and designs have not been documented anywhere, by anyone, until now. At the same time, I must admit that I cannot stop picturing myself down in the basement of Library and Archives Canada, crouching above the unlabelled, dusty box, and holding for the first time that glowing pile of reel-to-reel tapes in my hands, the mummified corpse of a long-lost love. I am about to initiate a world-historical drama that has been plotted across the stars for centuries. On the horizon are verdant bounties of uncollected materials, and traversed yet improperly charted territories; glistening and nearly impossible machines, plus unfathomable networks and storage formats; dear, faithful, generous collaborators; and, most voluptuously of all, trounced lickspittles capable of connecting nothing with nothing, treading in the fluxing backwash brought forth by my labours. This image brings me great pleasure. And the feelings of pride and power evoked by this scenario are significant if the reader of the present text is to understand the position that I have played in Canadian folk song collection.[7]

---

5   In fact, the box fell onto the floor after I was already several steps past, on account, I believe, of having been filed away by my often too-hasty fellow intern, Steven. For rhetorical purposes, however, I have preferred the classical eureka moment metaphor and have evoked it often in my lectures and presentations.

6   See, for example, Terry Seguin, *Information Morning*, CBC Radio One, 2003–Present, Fredericton.

7   This rhetorical play is known by sociologists as the self-fulfilling prophecy: "If men [sic] define situations as real, they are real in their consequences." William Isaac Thomas and Dorothy Swaine Thomas, *The Child in America: Behavior Problems and Programs* (New York, NY: Knopf, 1928), 571–572.

HORSEMAN[8]

I'm a horseman running ahead of the light.
I'm a fortress moving against the night.
My back is broken and my muscles are torn,
But in the wake of my body moves a shelter.

I prayed for strength and I am strong.
I prayed for love and I belong on this field.
I prayed for courage and I am courageous.
I am a sword, and the lord is my shield.

Sing low, sweet chariot, coming for to carry me home.
Sing low, sweet chariot, coming for to carry me home.

My brothers and I, we join hands.
We put our heads down, and we pump our legs.
I am the slowest but I will keep up.
In the wake of our bodies moves a shelter.

I prayed for strength and we're strong.
I prayed for love, and we belong on this field.
I prayed for courage and we are courageous.
In the wake of our bodies moves a shelter.

---

8 In the Book of Revelation, the Four Horsemen of the Apocalypse burst onto Armageddon with well-known fury and energy. On the other hand, in Canadian football the "horsemen" instead clear a path for the kickoff or punt returner: after the ball is launched by a kicker, four players assemble—on some teams and at some levels even holding hands to establish their connectivity and immovableness—and then move forward with an unfathomable solidity and, but perhaps it is the same thing, solidarity. See Evelyn Bloch, *The Language(s) of Canadian Sport(s)* (Regina, SK: University of Regina Press, 1995).

THE RAMBLIN' BOY

Given that academic folklore is a relatively young discipline, and considering that this young discipline has still not quite established itself within the university as its postwar pioneers had hoped, I am surprised at how elitist many contemporary folklorists are in relation to their field.[9] "Who are you under?" I heard my folklorist colleagues ask with suspicion more than once during the scheduled coffee breaks at the annual International Association for the Study of Folk Music conference, the one time I attended. In the parlance of the folklorists, "being under" means studying or having studied with a particular mentor, thus having been imprinted by a particular pedigree; the question is a means of quickly establishing connections, lineages, and allegiances in the competitive marketplace of ideas.[10] Of course, the question also ordains the policing of boundaries, since not everyone making major contributions is or has been *under* anyone. I, for example, despite my profound contributions, lack professional training as a folklorist.

It would be a lie, however, to state that I did not have experience in the field of practical, commercial folk song presentation. Because one sweltering July, at the age of twenty-four, I volunteered in Gannat, France, at one of Europe's largest traditional music festivals. The experience would profoundly mark my trajectory as a future folk song collector.

Founded in 1973, Les Cultures du Monde was, in the early days, a small gathering where one imagines moccasin-wear-

---

9 The first North American folklore department was established in Indiana in 1949. There are currently only two PhD programs in folklore in Canada, one of them focusing exclusively on Ukrainian folklore. For a personal, subjective analysis of the American context, see William A. Wilson, "Building Bridges: Folklore in the Academy," *Journal of Folklore Research* 33, no. 1 (1996): 7–14.

10 Paul Blackmore and Camille B. Kandiko, "Motivation in Academic Life: A Prestige Economy," *Research in Post-Compulsory Education* 16, no. 4 (2011): 399–411.

ing college kids swapping "Kumbaya" or perhaps even "Frère Jacques" on vintage accordions.[11] A few of these elderly visionaries were still involved when I attended. But by 2006, the annual ritual had been scaled up to corporatized proportions; deploying hundreds of volunteers and artists, organizers expected over twenty-five thousand visitors and four hundred musicians and dancers over the course of the two-week-long event. The operation had become a masterful combination of modern command and control, with a dash of good old-fashioned alchemy: a machine that could convert love—the universal love of folk music—directly into surplus profits and capital growth.[12]

My discrete role in the assembly line was as follows: In exchange for a dormitory bed and two square meals per day, I worked as translator and guide for the eight-piece Slovakian folk symphony Politran. It was my function to accompany the band on their daytrips to surrounding villages, where they performed melancholic melodies on violins, pipes, and cimbalom while dressed in traditional Slovakian garb.[13] Responsible for liaising between the venue technicians and Pavel, the octogenarian bandleader, as stages were set and any post-concert arrangements made, I served as a kind of medium.

On one occasion, our party was divided into pairs and ferried to home-cooked dinners scattered across a small village, where we had earlier that day played the annual street car-

---

11 It is clear, then, that the folk music revival was a distinctly international movement. To scratch the surface of this complexity, see Robert Cantwell, *When We Were Good: The Folk Revival* (Cambridge, MA: Harvard University Press, 1993); Ronald D. Cohen and Rachel Clare Donaldson, *Roots of the Revival: American and British Folk Music in the 1950s* (Champaign, IL: University of Illinois Press, 2014); Gillian Mitchell, *The North American Folk Revival: Nation and Identity in the United States and Canada, 1945-1980* (Burlington, VT: Ashgate Pub, 2016).

12 See Nick Dyer-Witheford, "Cybernetics and the Making of a Global Proletariat," *The Political Economy of Communication* 4, no. 1 (2016): 35–65.

13 The cimbalom is an ancient Eastern European folk piano. Rather than pressing keys, the player strikes the strings directly with mallets. For a history of this fascinating tool, see Jesse A. Johnston, "The Cimbál (Cimbalom) and Folk Music in Moravian Slovakia and Valachia," *Journal of the American Musical Instrument Society* 36 (2010): 78–117. Politran's cimbalom weighed hundreds of pounds and required five people to move—which, in Gannat, often included me.

nival. This was probably in Saint-Bonnet-de-Rochefort. I was partnered with a shy teenager, Susan, with whom I enjoyed a dinner of barely seared steaks and buttery beans. "C'est très bien," I said more than once to our hosts, Anne and Martin, on behalf of us both. After dessert, we went to the garden for digestifs, where our hosts' precocious French child interrogated me about my reading habits amid dark vines and flat stones. Anne asked Susan what initially had drawn her to traditional music, to which Susan responded, through me, "the music."The hitherto quiet grandmother posed questions too, which I was unable to answer, about Quebec.

But when the last herbaceous drops were swallowed and the night seemed finally to have floundered to an end, there was a sudden explosion of singing. Peter and Josef. We could hear the two rowdy boys belting out ancient anthems from maybe a mile away, drunk on *slivovice* and perhaps also the irrepressible joy of life, their voices carried like smoke signals by the thick, summery night.[14] I interpreted a pang of disappointment behind the tired smiles of our hosts. I understood they had wanted such exuberance and exoticism out of the evening, but had instead gotten stuck with the shy band member and, worse, the Canadian.

In any case, it was my responsibility to convey to the band when certain sequences, like meals, were about to happen. I took this role seriously. For in the field of commercial folk song presentation, as on the field of Canadian football, there are no small positions; there are only small players.

---

14 "In communist society, where nobody has one exclusive sphere of activity but each can become accomplished in any branch he wishes, society regulates the general production and thus makes it possible for me to do one thing today and another tomorrow, to hunt in the morning, fish in the afternoon, rear cattle in the evening, criticize after dinner, just as I have a mind, without ever becoming hunter, fisherman, herdsman or critic." Karl Marx and Friedrich Engels, *Collected Works, Volume 5* (New York, NY: International Publishers, 1976), 47. Although technically they were professional musicians, the gutterality and irrepressibility of Peter's and Josef's voices taught me about this category of collectivist liberty months before I was to encounter young Marx's words.

LE VRAI TAMBOUR[15]

Nous marchons,
Nous marchons,
Nous marchons ensemble !

Nos adversaires,
Adversaires,
Nos adversaires tremblent !

Nous mangeons,
Nous mangeons,
Nous mangeons ensemble !

Nos adversaires,
Adversaires,
Nos adversaires tremblent !

Et mon amour,
Mon amour,
Mon amour, elle me donnera...

Un gros bisou !

Parce que...

Nous avons le vrai tambour !

---

15   The (intentional) paucity of information regarding where and when, exactly,
Livingston recorded each song in his Sessions is in no way ameliorated in the
case of the French-language performances; French-Canadian football players
are as likely to be playing for Montreal as, for example, Vancouver. Charles
Gluck, "'Drop-Kick Me, Jesus': Religion, Faith, Language, and Ethnicity in the
Canadian Football League," *The International Journal of the History of Sports* 19,
no. 10 (2002): 1374–1397.

HURRAH, LIE!

While it contributed to my development as a responsible citizen of the world, my time in Gannat can also be scoured for direct impressions related to my emerging critical conceptualization of folk song. First, I was fascinated by the festival's promotional campaign, which promised world music connoisseurs a veritable smorgasbord of sounds, dances, and costumes. The real things. Introductory speeches by MCs or artistic directors—in the gigantic mainstage tent, or in the smaller venues, such as the church or gazebo—highlighted the authenticity of the performers. "Ce groupe de musiciens camerounais n'avait jamais pris l'avion la semaine dernière," a tall man with a moustache declared as he paced in pensive amazement. Or, as a local DJ between acts exclaimed, "Ce groupe norvégien n'a jamais été payé pour ses performances, jusqu'à maintenant!" Delicately munching on savory snacks, the names of which have escaped me, the mostly white bourgeois audience would gasp rapturously, ready to receive sounds uncorrupted by technology or "time-space compression"; uncorrupted, in other words, by postmodernity.[16]

I want to make clear that the festival's primitivist articulation of authentic folk song was not the one that I was coming to adopt—then, or ever.[17] What intrigued me was the marked tension between the world of "the folk" according to Les

---

16 According to Marxist geographer David Harvey, "time-space compression" describes the complex socio-historical transformations wrought by the emergence of the post-Fordist paradigm and its correspondingly flexible techniques of capital accumulation. David Harvey, *The Condition of Postmodernity* (New York, NY: Blackwell, 1989), 284–307.

17 One of the most incisive critiques of which remains the following succinct statement by musician Big Bill Broonzy: "I guess all songs is folk songs. I never heard no horse sing 'em." Big Bill Broonzy quoted in Robin D. G. Kelley, "Notes on Deconstructing 'The Folk,'" *The American Historical Review* 97, no. 5 (1992): 1403.

Cultures du Monde, and the world as shared by the actual artists themselves. For every night, after the final concerts had sounded out, I would stop by the after-hours party organized as a perk for the performers and volunteers, where there was drinking, dancing, and merriment. This was happening in a backstage area, which meant that here one could acquire a sense of the interests and proclivities of the diverse labourers gathered for the festival without the demands of their public-facing, external masks.[18] Accordingly, conversations between musicians about geopolitical manouveurings and pop stars, about cinema and fashion, could be overheard; exhausted dancers arriving with Discman devices, or taking synthetic drugs in the restrooms, could be seen; and the early signals of extramarital sexual encounters could faintly be detected.[19] This is to say that the festival's authentic folk were not outside of postmodernity, but rather on the vanguard, looking both backward and forward simultaneously.[20]

Hence, when the festival director and co-founder Jean, in his trademark leather fedora, a veritable *petit* Indiana Jones, asked all translators and guides to inform their bands that artists were no longer permitted to smoke on festival grounds while still in costume, so that the sanctity of the simulacrum on offer might be better preserved, I refused to pass on the message.[21] "They want you to smoke more!" I in fact said, to which the members of Politran only laughed and shrugged their shoulders. They too were beginning to tire of the peculiar paranoia of the French.

---

18 See Erving Goffman, *The Presentation of Self in Daily Life* (Norwell, MA: Anchor Books, 1959).

19 Regretfully, I made a tactical blunder by attempting to woo a redheaded Finnish kantele player who turned out to be a Pentecostal fundamentalist. "All I need is Jesus," beautiful Päivi said when, after a week of flirtation and long walks through the countryside, I had found an opportunity for us to kiss. See Kimberly Ervin Alexander, "Pentacostal Women: Chosen for an Exalted Destiny," *Theology Today* 68, no. 4 (2012): 404–412.

20 Walter Benjamin, *Illuminations*, trans. Harry Zohn (New York, NY: Shorcken Books, 1968), 253–264.

21 See Jean Baudrillard, *Simulacra and Simulation* (Ann Arbor, MI: University of Michigan press, 1994).

I'ZE THE BYE

In terms of technique, I was not a good translator of French to Slovak, or Slovak to French, it must be admitted. Consequently, I was responsible for some comic scenarios. For example, in one tiny hamlet, perhaps Le Mayet-d'École, the villagers and their mayor had gathered in the town square to present to Politran a copy of the key to their clock tower. A lovely gesture, and a well-attended ceremony. I was asked to translate, to convey to Politran the gist of the mayor's warm yet succinct gratitude, but when Pavel offered his response, which I was required to convey to both the mayor and the entire village, the linguistic mechanism in my mind all but seized.[22] Pavel's words were like slippery, Slovakian logs, bobbing and floating down a cold black stream, as I struggled to keep my head above water.[23] At a certain point, I must admit, I stopped even trying to follow his meaning.

What else could I have done? Not wanting to dampen or disrupt the festivities, when Pavel passed the microphone back, I simply reimagined the rules of the situation. I took a meditative beat and became *homo faber*, offering a detail-rich anecdote about the group's origins in the ghettoes of Bratislava; an excursion about how two of the band members had fallen in love—against their parents' wishes—as they first began, together, to explore the performance of traditional music; and the climax of my monologue, which was that, through all their

---

22 My interpreters deploying Propp's Morphology may wish to draw their attention to the villainy or lacking motifs, in which the hero discovers that they are suddenly without a key potion or weapon at a decisive moment. Vladimir Propp, *Morphology of the Folk Tale*, trans. Laurence Scott (Austin, TX: University of Austin Press, 1968), 30–36.

23 Which clearly foreshadows my looming vocational transition, given the significance of the "cold black stream" in Canadian folkloristics. See, for example, Edith Fowke, *Lumbering Songs from the Northern Woods* (Toronto, ON: NC Press, 1985).

days of study and rehearsal, Politran had only ever had one dream, that being to come to France to share their traditional music and lore. I imagined these statements as oak logs in a cabin that I was both making and subsequently inhabiting. When I finally knotted it together with a joke about how all of Canada is a frozen wasteland, there was a standing ovation.

Thus, I learned many lessons in Gannat related to folk song theory and praxis. Nonetheless, what I remember most of all from that time is the music, which remains glorious. There was one afternoon gig at a pizza parlour in particular. Because the place was empty, the owner had suggested the orchestra assemble outside the restaurant, on the street, so that passersby at least could enjoy the music; but ominous clouds meant that I was, even then, the only auditor in attendance. As the soft mists fell from the darkening sky onto our medieval alleyway, as the winds began warmly to gust—and as I ate with my hands the delicious *morceau* of blueberry flan purchased across the street, a new-world barbarian, practically swimming in my faded cords and frayed button-down—Politran played with an intensity I had not yet heard. It was as though their flesh and mine were glowing, fire. At one point, the heavy cimbalom, plunking and planking in its characteristically mournful manner, began to take on the contours of a powder keg.[24]

I can grasp now that these Slovakian folk virtuosos were not playing for me. However, I was there. And although I did not yet have the tools with which I might have captured Politran's eternal, incandescent cries, it is possible that I have been chasing them ever since.

---

24 "In literature the term [synesthesia] is applied to descriptions of one kind of sensation in another." M. H. Abrams, *A Glossary of Literary Terms, Seventh Edition* (New York, NY: Harcourt Brace College Publishers, 1985), 315. In folk song, however, as my experience attests, synesthetic perception is possible without any descriptions at all.

THE BOLD ROUGHRIDER[25]

They smelled like perfume, sweat 'n' ketchup.
They felt like a diner feels after the bar.
I'm so far from my home.
But no one needs to be alone.

And my body feels like hurting and bleeding,
And chopping,[26]
And getting knocked down.
My life has not been easy.
But these legs will carry me.

As I go down this road,
I'll leave you some signposts.
They'll tell you where I've loved and been,
And what I've seen.
Please see they're kept clean.

---

25 During the 1960s and 1970s, there were two CFL teams who incorporated "rough riding" into their brand—the Saskatchewan Roughriders and the Ottawa Rough Riders. In fact, the Rough Riders and the Roughriders coexisted in the Canadian Football League from 1958 until 1996 when the Ottawa team folded. They even faced off in the 1976 Grey Cup championship game, with the Rough Riders out-steering the Roughriders 23-20. It is considered by many to have been the most exciting game in CFL history, and, by me, as the most beautiful. It is also the final CFL game that Staunton R. Livingston would have been able to watch in his short life.

26 The "chop" or "cut" block is a specific technique in the game of Canadian football whereby the blocking player directs their energy downwards—to the thigh, knee, shin, or ankle region of the defender. This move is particularly useful for players who lack size or strength in comparison to the opposing player whose path they are striving to obstruct. Due to the high level of injury risk involved in chopping or cutting, the NFL has banned the practice since the 2016–2017 season. See Danny Kelly, "Here's What the NFL's New Chop Block Rule Really Means," SBNation.com, March 23, 2016. It remains common and legal, however, in the Canadian Football League, so long as performed within particular parameters, which I do not have the space to explore here.

CHUG ALL NIGHT

While my acquaintances from undergrad moved to Montreal to spend their nights doing bumps of powdery drugs at the corner tables of Saint Laurent dives, I chose to feast on the psychotropic buffet of propositions known as graduate school in the humanities. Within a few short weeks, after my late-August return from Europe, I had already added to my lexicon such terms as *abjection, affect, capital, desiring-machine, diaspora, Orientalism, subculture, phallus,* and *hegemony*.[27]

However, whereas some of my new colleagues and mentors saw education as a single school of thought—there was the ritual marriage (the thesis defense), and the endless production of identical offspring (research paper after research paper, with slight tweaks to the basic insights in light of new texts or trends)—I would instead come to see myself as a conceptual circuit bender, connecting and soldering, rewiring, and modulating.[28] There would be no marriage, at least

---

27 See, respectively, Julia Kristeva, *Powers of Horror* (New York, NY: Columbia University Press, 1984); Brian Massumi, *Parables for the Virtual: Movement, Affect, Sensation* (Durham, NC: Duke University Press, 2002); Karl Marx, *Capital: A Critique of Political Economy*, trans. Ben Fowkes (New York, NY: Vintage Books, 1977); Gilles Deleuze and Félix Guattari, *Anti-Oedipus: Capitalism and Schizophrenia*, trans. Robert Hurley, Mark Seem, and Helen R. Lane (Minneapolis, MN: University of Minnesota Press, 1983); Paul Gilroy, *The Black Atlantic: Modernity and Double Consciousness* (Cambridge, MA: Harvard University Press, 1993); Edward Said, *Orientalism* (New York, NY: Pantheon Books, 1978); Dick Hebdige, *Subculture: The Meaning of Style* (New York, NY: Routledge, 1979); Jacques Lacan, *Écrits* (Milton: Taylor & Francis, 2012); Antonio Gramsci, *Selections from the Prison Notebooks* (New York, NY: International Publishers, 1971).

28 This might be read in one of two ways. First, there was a generous pragmatism brewing in my thinking as I became initiated into the university life, an openness to practically infinite ways of doing and being. See Gilles Deleuze and Félix Guattari, *A Thousand Plateaus: Capitalism and Schizophrenia*, trans. Brian Massumi (Minneapolis, MN: University of Minnesota Press, 1987). And second, there was an irrepressible independence, a constant refusal to be contained or controlled by any one tradition or school. See Jeremiah 2:20, New International Version.

not right away, because it was not one idea after which I was questing. It was every one of them.

The only reason I applied to the University of Western Ontario in the first place was that I had a place to stay in town: a psychology clinic—the Institute—in a building owned by my father, where an unoccupied and rent-free apartment lay dormant in the basement. In some respects, this was not ideal. Stained, dusty carpets, low ceilings, no light. The upper levels of the old Victorian house were clean and bright, but the basement—the only part to which I had access—was a vestige of the building's former years as a fraternity residence and had not been inhabited, updated, or cleaned for at least two decades.[29] But the University of Western Ontario offered funding packages for graduate students in the Communication Studies program, which meant that, if I stayed at the Institute, I could drink and eat well for a man in his twenties, take the train to Toronto sometimes on the weekends, and devote myself completely to my studies. I could walk the path along the verdant Thames river floodplain to campus. I could score the odd free lunch from my father. Indeed, in several respects I expected this to be a happy, peaceful, and productive time in my life, at least at the start.

It would be fascinating from a scholarly perspective to re-watch my first meeting with Dr. Cameron Bronnley. I recall a grey flannel suit playfully deconstructed by light blue sneakers, a bottle of Scotch on his bookshelf, and his bald head; I was likely dressed as a farmer, in shapeless dark-brown chinos and a faded flannel shirt, an untrimmed beard.[30] But

---

29 I often wondered whether this basement had not been used primarily for archaic hazing practices, which are forms of folklore in their own right. Jay Mechling, "Is Hazing Play?," *Transactions at Play* 9 (2009): 45–61.

30 My maternal grandfather was a farmer, as well as a tall and brawny man; earlier that spring, upon his passing, I had inherited from him a large plastic bag full of rustic clothes, which became my primary garments from 2006–12. Albeit unawares, I would therefore come to participate in a longstanding tradition: See M.A. Kucherskaya, "Wearing Folk Costumes as a Mimetic Practice in Russian Ethnographic Field Studies," *Archaeology, Ethnology & Anthropology of Eurasia* 47, no. 1 (2019): 127–136.

what was on my mind? My initial thesis proposal focused on paradigms of labour and self-presentation in American method acting; Dr. Bronnley, given his area of expertise, had thus been a logical choice to serve as mentor.[31] But how did I see myself, my situation? How did Dr. Bronnley see me, and how did his gaze affect the intellectual path on which I was about to embark? An analysis of both my words and body language in that first meeting, in comparison to my words and body language now, might indicate the degree to which academic professionalization can seep into one's synapses.

By even posing these questions, however, I reveal the degree to which it is difficult to refrain from forcing contemporary ways of thinking, acquired through gradual processes of sedimentation, onto past actions and experiences.[32] Techniques and modes acquired from Dr. Bronnley have no doubt inflected (infected?) even the manners by which I might try to analyze these very influences. This is evident in the structure, in the syntax, and in the citations of the present text. It is tough to become free, as G. F. W. Hegel was perhaps the first to observe.[33]

Epistemological quandaries aside, I do know that the early stages of my research conducted under Dr. Bronnley's guidance were fruitful. As a younger man, I had entertained ideals of art as autonomous, yet my new teacher was pressing me to consider how taste could be both historical and, in certain cultural fields, a complex weapon of distinct class

---

31 Although his recent publication history was scant, Bronnley had made a name for himself with a widely cited essay on the performative conventions of televised celebrity talk show programs. Cameron Bronnley, "Hi, Dave: Repetition, Reversal, and Dialogism on Late-Night TV," *Cultural and Social Texts* 32, no. 3 (1991): 1204–1227.

32 Félix Guattari, *Chaosmosis: An Ethico-Aesthetic Paradigm* (Bloomington, IN: Indiana University Press, 1994).

33 G. W. F. Hegel, *The Phenomenology of Spirit*, translated by Peter Fuss and John Dobbins (Notre Dame, IN: University of Notre Dame Press, 2019)

strata.[34] Authenticity, for example, which is the ultimate goal of the method actor who draws on their individual wounds and traumas in the service of theatrical art, was not natural or self-evident; the concept was rather a complex hallucination emanating from particular petit bourgeois worldviews within modern mass societies, something about which I had already formed suspicions in Gannat.[35] It followed that in order to study rigorously authentic art or performance, one was required not only to behold the artworks or performances themselves through close reading techniques, but also to examine the processes of legitimation—involving practices of concepts such as criticism, celebrity, authorship, owner-ship, publicity, promotion, nationalism, scholarship, and so on—that enveloped the aesthetic object in question.[36] I am not sure that I would have been able to arrive at the present

---

34 The first text along these lines that Bronnley suggested, if memory serves, is Pierre Bourdieu, *Distinction: A Social Critique of the Judgment of Taste* (Cam-bridge, MA: Harvard University Press, 1984).

35 Theodor W. Adorno, *The Jargon of Authenticity* (Evanston, IL: University if Illi-nois Press, 1973). See also, for example, Simon Frith, "'The Magic That Can Set You Free': The Ideology of Folk and the Myth of the Rock Community," *Popular Music* 1 (1981): 159–68; Lawrence Grossberg, *We Gotta Get Out of This Place: Popular Conservatism and Postmodern Culture* (New York, NY: Routledge, 1992); Alison Hearn, "John, A 20-year-old Boston Native with a Great Sense of Humour: On the Spectacularization of the Self and the Incorporation of Iden-tity in the Age of Reality Television," *International Journal of Media & Cultural Politics* 2, no. 2 (2006): 131-147; Keir Keightley, "Reconsidering Rock," in *The Cambridge Companion to Pop and Rock*, eds. Simon Frith, William Straw, John Street (Cambridge, UK: Cambridge University Press, 2001), 109–142; Richard Sennett, *The Fall of Public Man* (New York, NY: W.W. Norton, 1974).

36 See also Jody Berland, *North of Empire: Essays on the Cultural Technologies of Space* (Durham, NC: Duke University Press, 2009); Richard Dyer, *Stars* (London: British Film Institute, 1979); Paul Gilroy, *"There Ain't No Black in the Union Jack": The Cultural Politics of Race and Nation* (London: Hutchinson, 1987); P. David Marshall, *Celebrity and Power: Fame in Contemporary Culture* (Minneapolis, MN: University of Minnesota Press, 2014); Richard A. Peterson, *Creating Country Music: Fabricating Authenticity* (Chicago, IL: University of Chi-cago Press, 2013); Jonathan Sterne, *The Audible Past: Cultural Origins of Sound Reproduction* (Durham, NC: Duke University Press, 2003).

text without having been guided through these initial, heavy discoveries by Dr. Bronnley.

In terms of the rhythms and patterns of daily life, on the other hand, the first two years at Western were relatively friction-free sailing. A round of beers after class, often at my instigation, could turn into several, and then into cab rides downtown, where I would drink and debate in one of the dimly lit taverns apparently unknown to undergraduates until last call. I enjoyed these spirited sessions with or without my classmates. And there was sometimes cash left over to treat the hangovers at my local greasy spoon, Campus Hi-Fi, the name of which alluded to that technological phylum beginning with Thomas Alva Edison's phonograph and continuing through to artificially intelligent musical machines.[37] I wonder even now: Was proximity to this establishment destiny's way of foreshadowing?

I must confess that I was additionally settling into the gothic grandeur of London. This was actually, aside from a past spring when I had hitchhiked to Vancouver to work as a motion picture background performer, my first time living in a proper city, a genre of civilizational assembly about which I had formerly been somewhat suspicious, on aesthetic if not ethical or political grounds. Whether it was the particular stop-and-go of traffic or the general hum of observable decay, or the incessant deception and theatricality of all social life, most urban settings made me, from an early age, especially anxious.[38] And yet, apparently one's sensorium can be trans-

---

37 In addition to letting you substitute pancakes for toast, at Campus Hi-Fi they always had a pleasant mix of classic rock hits playing softly on the stereo. On the relationship between place and broadcast radio, see Jody Berland, "Radio Space and Industrial Time: Music Formats, Local Narratives and Technological Mediation," *Popular Music* 9.2 (1990): 179–192.

38 Of course, although they can be traced back to Jean-Jacques Rousseau, these sentiments are not uncommon in the Canadian folklore scene. Dale Ricks, for example, often decries the "noises" encountered in the urban song-collecting milieu. E.g., Dale Ricks, "Some Songs of Winnipeg," *Canadian Journal of Folkloristics* 103, no. 1 (2012): 51-72. Unlike Ricks, I am at least trying to be honest, self-reflexive, and ultimately critical about this shared positionality.

formed. Indeed, despite the constant noise, or maybe because of it, I was to my surprise becoming enamoured with the long, broad thoroughfares, the arboreous parks and lawns, and the obviously haunted mansions of the city.[39]

Time off campus was spent downtown, where I had my rituals. I would buy a latte and butter tart, work upstairs in the Covent Garden Market, and wander on breaks through the urban blight of dilapidated Dundas Street to absorb the aura of the very same *Lumpenproletariat* about which I had been reading so much.[40] Finally, the long walk home: up along the meandering Thames, past vast fields of geese and shit, through wooded stretches and flourishing floral groves. They called London the Forest City, in part because of this unique collapsing of margin and centre.[41] And, in my view, it is now indeed the most beautiful city in Southwestern Ontario, if not the entire world.

There was at first not much dating or sex, however, perhaps because of the decrepitude of my living situation. There had been, in addition to the deficiencies sketched above, a flood at the end of my first autumn at the Institute, from which the greyish-brown basement carpet never quite recovered. It is also worth pointing out that I was, at this time, missing my two bottom-front incisors.[42] However, in those days it

---

39   Another fortuitous bit of foreshadowing, given the centrality of ghost stories within Canadian folklore. See, for instance, Helen Creighton, *Bluenose Ghosts* (Toronto, ON: Ryerson University Press, 1957).

40   Walter Benjamin, *Illuminations*, trans. Harry Zohn (New York, NY: Schocken Books, 1968), 217–252.

41   Poles of modernity known in sociology as *Gemeinschaft* and *Gesellschaft*. Ferdinand Tönnies, *Community and Civil Society*, trans. Jose Harris and Margaret Hollis (New York, NY: Cambridge University Press, 2001).

42   My denticles departed as the result of a sucker punch earlier that year, in February, in Halifax, Nova Scotia. I was in a heated argument with the friend I was visiting at the time, regarding the correct definition and application of *defamiliarization*. I stared at my friend and said, "I dare you to hit me," in response to which he exited the public house. Minutes later, although I was sitting peacefully on a barstool, unprotected and unbraced, I found myself suddenly on the floor: a sidewinding hook, *ex nihilo*. Coincidentally,

was as though all carnal propulsions had been transposed or translated, if not entirely neutered. I was cruising, not the shopping mall or boardwalk, but the library stacks, a horny bibliographer thirsting after all germane graphic materials.[43] Hard or soft, damaged or clean, print or DVD—no matter. At one point, I had more than 120 items on loan from the university library, for which I was eventually shamed at the circulation desk, one supposes justifiably.[44]

Therefore, when I first read the call for applications to spend part of the summer working at Library and Archives Canada in Ottawa as an intern, I found the prospect titillating. I did not see myself surrounded by new or interesting people—all other people were either dead or very far away in this fantasy—but by long rows of rich, voluptuous documents. Ensconced by smoldering letters and spirits. Primary responsibilities included the appraisal, description, and arrangement of donations to the sound and video recording fonds. Thus, I wrote a short letter of interest highlighting the social significance of audio-visual cultural memory, secured a letter of recommendation from Dr. Bronnley, and landed the gig.[45] My first professional triumph.

I remembered later that the line—"I dare you to hit me"—is something that, as a boy, I had heard one of my father's old football buddies recount while telling a story about their roughhousing days. I'm not sure why it came to me then, but it is fascinating, indeed, the power that folk songs and stories have to shape our minds and worlds—and mouths. Roland Barthes, *Mythologies*, trans. Annette Lavers (New York, NY: Hill and Wang, 1972).

43 Jacques Derrida has offered a name for this hot affliction: "archive fever." Jacques Derrida, *Archive Fever: A Freudian Impression*, trans. Eric Prenowitz (Chicago, IL: University of Chicago Press, 1995).

44 Nonetheless, I was defiant in my right to acquire infinite texts from the library, rhetorically asking the circulation desk attendant, after his sassy reprimand, whether he would like also to make comments about my usage of the postal system. It is important that citizens in a democratic society have free access to clear channels of communication. Robert W. McChesney, *Rich Media, Poor Democracy: Communication Politics in Dubious Times* (New York, NY: The New Press, 2016).

45 I drew in particular on Marita Sturken, *Tangled Memories* (Berkeley, CA: University of California Press, 1997).

In fact, it was Dr. Bronnley who had sent me the advertisement for the internship in the first place. He had gotten into the habit of forwarding peer-reviewed articles or opportunities that he thought related to my research interests, which I can see now was intended as a subtle form of domination. "FYI," these short missives would read, followed by several links. From Bronnley's point of view, such an internship would have helped me to build my resumé, which would have helped me to land a competitive postdoctoral fellowship, which would have helped me to join the professoriate and, ultimately, to publish articles in which I would cite my supervisors, including one Dr. C. Bronnley. It was a pseudo-Ponzi scheme propped up by the malleability of young minds.

Of course, Dr. Bronnley could not have known that this opportunity would, on the contrary, lead to a severing of our relationship, due to the inevitable personal paradigm shift resulting from my discovery of Staunton R. Livingston's epic masterpiece, the CFL Sessions, the authentic work of art I uncovered in the basement of Library and Archives Canada.[46] Which is exactly what was about to happen.

---

46 Paradigms are static, seemingly universal structures, but only until they crumble back to dust, from which new paradigms often emerge after either prolonged or brief—though often bloody—battle. Thomas S. Kuhn, *The Structure of Scientific Revolutions* (Chicago, IL: University of Chicago Press, 1962).

LIFE IS LIKE CANADIAN FOOTBALL

Life is like Canadian football, you don't get many chances.[47]
But there's a lot of room to move around.[48]
Life's like Canadian football, there aren't too many teams.[49]
So, just pick the one that's closest to your heart
And scream for them.

Life is like Canadian football, it's like
Life is like Canadian football, it's like life:
There's a lot of room to move around.

Life is like Canadian football;
It's not always televised.[50]
So, take those moments by the hand,
You can't rewind.

Life is like Canadian football;
We got this thing called the rouge.[51]
So, unless you take chances sometimes, you're going to lose.

---

47 The offense is only given three opportunities or "downs" to advance ten yards, at which point, if successful, they receive a new set of downs. If unsuccessful, the other team's offense assumes control. In American football there are four downs. Anonymous, "Down (Gridiron Football)," Wikipedia.

48 In Canadian college and professional football, the field is significantly larger than in the American variation, by 10 yards in length and 11.67 yards in width. See Anonymous, "Canadian Football Field," Wikipedia; Anonymous, "American Football Field," Wikipedia.

49 There are currently only nine teams in total.

50 This is perhaps, at time of writing, no longer true. See Robert Sparks, "'Delivering the Male': Sports, Canadian Television, and the Making of TSN," *Canadian Journal of Communication* 17, no. 3 (1992): 319–342.

51 The "rouge" is a single point, which can be scored by kicking the ball through the opponent's end zone, or by your opponent's giving up a touchback within their own end zone. There are no rouges in the American variation of the game of football. There are also no Wikipedia entries on the rouge.

Life is like Canadian football, you can't really make
    any money.
Just make sure you knock someone down and that you
    protect your buddies.
Life is like Canadian football;
You can either take a hit or you can't,
And there's a lot of room to move around.

NIGHT HERDING SONG

I have dreamt the following scene, which takes place in a locker room at dusk, players and coaches gone home save one, a second-string middle linebacker. Still wearing his sweat-salted tank top and grass-stained pants, and obviously exhausted, he sits on a long bench strewn with towels and half-full water bottles, odorous kneepads and jockstraps. He diligently tunes a scratched-up guitar while an older man, with sideburns and long hair, sets up a large condenser microphone, a delicate instrument in its own right. After unspooling the cables and positioning the stand, the phonographer stands back by his reel-to-reel tape recorder, propped solidly on a parallel bench, and, after a moment of meditation, inspects his informant. The player halts his restless, shaking knee. And then: A song emerges in the key of G. It is about the essential desire of humanity to create both the world and itself; hence, it is a song about everything that it is possible to sing.[52] And it is beautiful. The vibrations move throughout the cavernous space, swelling and surging, expanding and contracting. Converted into analogous electrical waves by the microphone, the signal sears like an endlessly burning cigarette straight onto the humming tape. By the end of the second refrain, the phonographer has begun, silently, to weep.

It remains unclear why Staunton R. Livingston chose to record songs of Canadian football players in the 1970s.[53]

---

52 Ernst Bloch, *The Principle of Hope*, trans. Neville Plaice, Stephen Plaice, and Paul Knight (Oxford: B. Blackwell, 1986).

53 There were precedents. As is well known, John and Alan Lomax in 1933 took their 300-pound Dictaphone on the road throughout the Deep South, stopping at work camps and prisons in order to collect American folk songs. The Lomaxes thought such sites could serve as de facto reservoirs of authentic folk-musical culture, in part because of the strict boundaries essentially imposed by those organizations. Benjamin Filene, *Romancing the Folk* (Chapel Hill, NC: University of North Carolina Press, 2000); Mary Beth Hamilton, *In Search of*

The most reasonable explanation I have yet invented centres on the fact that Canadian football is both a modernist and a traditional art. On one hand, the language of industrialized warfare saturates the game in terms of both mechanics and strategy. To list only a few examples, one throws the *long bomb*; one sends the *blitz*; the *line* itself—which must be held or advanced—is referred to as the *trenches*; the *division of labour*, including the differentiation between manual and intellectual work, precisely mirrors that of the Fordist factory system; and, of course, the muscular players in their shoulder pads and helmets, sprung coils of strength and speed and machinic armor, exactly resemble *Unique Forms of Continuity in Space* by the Italian Futurist Umberto Boccioni.[54] On the other hand, the reason the Canadian and American games of football are currently so divergent, despite sharing an identical historical origin point, is that the Canadian game's rules were changed more slowly and conservatively in order to preserve the original source of rugby, whereas the Americans quickly modified their version to suit advertisers and broadcast corporations.[55] Perhaps the Canadian Football League in and of itself appealed to Livingston—its mashup of present

the Blues: Black Voices, White Visions (New York, NY: Basic Books, 1998); Karl Hagstrom Miller, *Segregating Sound: Inventing Folk and Pop Music in the Age of Jim Crow* (Durham, NC: Duke University Press, 2010).

54 However, Boccioni's masterpiece pales in comparison, if I may be so bold, to the aesthetic shimmer of a tight end pulverizing a defensive back on the sweep.

55 One of the consequences of these differences is that the Canadian game involves higher levels of movement, action, tension, and excitement than the American variation, despite the lower levels of capital, size, and spectacular commodification. On the historical development of the rules, conventions, and cultural significance of Canadian football, see John Nauright and Phil White, "Mediated Nostalgia, Community and Nation: The Canadian Football League in Crisis and the Demise of the Ottawa Rough Riders, 1986–1996," *Sport History Review* 33, no. 2 (2002): 121–137; Bob Sproule, "Canadian Football: Past to Present," *The Coffin Corner* 13, no. 1 (1991): 1–5; and Fred Wiseman, *A Frosty Game: The Glacial but Profound Changes in Canadian Football in the Twentieth Century* (Fredericton, NB: Goose Lane Editions, 1990).

and past, cutting edge and solid root—insofar as we can piece together his taste and disposition.

A relevant obstruction within the field of Livingston studies, however, is the fact that, after 1966, Staunton R. Livingston did not write anything down. This of course does not mean that he also refrained from thinking, or imparting. He was active in the fields of both ethnomusicology and folklore; although he was an independent, self-taught folklorist, Livingston presented research at major scholarly conferences between 1967 and 1971. Still, representation of Livingston's philosophy has come to us only through the writings of members of his audiences, the entirety of which has had a vested interest in discounting the integrity, cohesion, and revolutionary power of his ideas. All communication, even communication with one's self, involves the unavoidable distortions of noise.[56] Things get even messier when one's enemies are the ones writing the story.

I had not yet fully fleshed out these problematics when I first began to listen to the CFL Sessions in the summer of 2008. My internship at Library and Archives Canada had ended in late July, and I was in Toronto, having found a short-term sublet in Little Portugal in order to collect myself before my duties as a teaching assistant and student recommenced in September. I had managed, before leaving Ottawa, to digitize the entirety of the CFL Sessions under the radar of the institution's panoptic supervisory system, so that the evaluation and distribution of the project's cultural value could not be slowed by any bureaucratic plots.[57] So, every morning as I walked east along College Street, past the ancient shopkeepers sweeping or watering their stretches of sidewalk, the strong summer sun already beating down, I was thus able to listen through headphones to the folk songs of Canadian football players. And I was falling in love.

---

56 Claude Elwood Shannon, "Communication in the Presence of Noise," *Proceedings of the IRE* 37, no. 1 (1949): 10-21.

57 See Gilles Deleuze, "Postscript on the Societies of Control," *October* 59 (1992): 3–7.

SONG WRITTEN UPON GETTING
CUT BY THE ARGOS

We could walk all night in this city
And still be in this city.
We could talk all night about leaving
And still be in this city.

I could drink all night in this city,
If we had any money.
Would you rather be sober and tired
Or drunk and bankrupt?[58]

We could dig all night in this city
And still be in this city.
We could dream of our home
And still be in this city.

I could drink all night in this city,
If we had any money.
Would you rather be sober and tired
Or drunk and bankrupt?

---

58   These exact words ("Would you rather be sober and tired or drunk and bankrupt?") were also spoken by Staunton R. Livingston himself in the attention-getting introduction of his final address to the Canadian Folkloristics Association, though we certainly cannot know if he had yet recorded "Song Written Upon Getting Cut By the Argos," or if he had even begun the CFL Sessions project. Peter Skellgord, "What I Can Remember," *Globe and Mail*, Dec 26, 1992, A4. Of course, it is possible that Livingston had heard but not yet recorded the song. There are other possibilities as well.

HAUL ON THE BOWLINE

It was to the St. George Campus at the University of Toronto that I was headed on those late-August mornings. Aside from brief lunches of banh mi and soda pop in Chinatown, I was spending the bulk of my days inside the Robarts Library.[59] It was quite symbolically in the belly—or perhaps gizzard—of that peacock-shaped horror that I felt my first glimmers of pride as a folk song collector, for I had found, and I had gathered, something of great cultural and political significance. At least, this was my conclusion after having completed an initial investigation into the life and work of Staunton R. Livingston.

My first lead was an article by Niles J. Paul Stanley in *The Encyclopedia of Canadian Folkloristics* entitled "Vagabondage," which is a folklore-specific term describing disciplinary interlopers. Reference to Livingston is made only in a footnote, a mere glancing blow; he appears in a three-item list of folk song collectors who have operated, according to Stanley, in compromising proximity to market imperatives, which is a preposterous claim in Livingston's case.[60] For the record, no real argument is made by Stanley; it appears as though the reader is expected to understand, before even having read the text, where it is that Livingston sits in relation to other so-called legitimate folklorists,

---

59 In 2008, as long as you were a graduate student in Ontario, it was still possible to acquire a complimentary pass to the University of Toronto library system. The same pass now costs $50, which is unfortunate given the drastic increases in average rent across the Greater Toronto Area, despite meagre gains in real wage growth in the region. See Sally Borden, *The Art of Economics and the Economics of Art: Making Work in Canada in the Twenty-First* Century (Montreal, QC: Black Rose Books, 2014).

60 Niles J. Paul Stanley, "Vagabondage," in *The Encyclopedia of Canadian Folkloristics*, ed. Denise LaFleur (Waterloo, ON: Wilfred Laurier Press, 1985), 761.

a rhetorical operation deplorably not uncommon in the discipline of folklore.[61]

A citation in Stanley's piece drew me to a second source, Rachel Alloway's *The Yorkville Scene and Environs*, an accessible oral history of various venues and clubs through which Livingston no doubt passed in the late sixties. Over the course of one and a half pages, Alloway sketches a disruptive set by Livingston at the Free Times Café, as well as Livingston's final scholarly presentation delivered in that same year, 1971, to the Canadian Folkloristics Association, in which he eviscerated the dominant regimes of Canadian folklore before declaring, by way of conclusion, both of his paper and of the scene: "I do not serve."[62] Alloway's text gives some indication of Livingston's attractive combination of musculature and grace; she claims he was approximately 250 pounds and yet moved through the world "like a hungry lion."[63] Regrettably, however, Livingston's radical commitments were intended by Alloway as comic relief within her otherwise competent, if also theoretically naive, monograph.

The deep reaches of the U of T computer databases allowed me to fill in additional events and developments. Livingston was born in 1936 in Windsor, Ontario, to working-class parents who laboured in either the whisky or automobile industries.[64] It is noted by Dane Spounge that he took an early interest in mathematics and military theory; it is additionally believed that, into his late teens, Livingston spent summers with a wealthy aunt and uncle on the Bruce

---

61 See also, for example, Richard Dorson, *Folklore and Fakelore* (Cambridge, MA: Harvard University Press, 1976).

62 Staunton R. Livingston quoted in Rachel Alloway, *The Yorkville Scene and Environs* (Nepean, ON: Borealis Press, 2001), 139.

63 Rachel Alloway, *The Yorkville Scene and Environs* (Nepean, ON: Borealis Press, 2001), 132.

64 There is some discrepancy on this point. See Peter Skellgord, "What I Can Remember," *Globe and Mail*, Dec 26, 1992, A4; and Paul Butterfield, "Infamous and Forgotten Windsorites," *Maclean's*, Dec 24, 2001, 37.

Peninsula, where he enjoyed observing fiddling contests.[65] A hardworking youth with voracious reading habits, he excelled in scholastics and was accepted to the University of Toronto, where he would study economics and political science on a full scholarship.[66]

But Livingston's performance and evolving mindset as an undergraduate become cloudier for the present-day historian. According to David Toogood, Livingston took two courses with Marshall McLuhan in 1954, ten full years before publication of the latter's landmark work *Understanding Media*, the central argument of which Toogood claims was strongly influenced by Livingston, though this claim seems intended as an insult toward both figures. "The bohemian long-haired spoken word poet from Windsor that [sic] student who invited McLuhan to soirees and séances [sic] was likely the English professor's guide into the mystical, hallucinatory delusions of the mid-career work on media," Toogood writes.[67] It is as though both Livingston and McLuhan are guilty by association, a logical fallacy which leads one to question the degree to which Toogood's narrative could be in any way otherwise accurate.

And the years 1960–67 are a complete blank. It is uncertain why Livingston arrested his studies just short of matriculation, or where he spent the mid-1960s. Fran Laney believes that Livingston went to New York City to immerse himself both in the booming American folk revival and in the interdisciplinary art scenes of Greenwich Village.[68] Polk Halkman

65 Dane Spounge, *The Origins of Canadian Beat and Spoken Word Poetry* (Regina, SK: University of Regina Press, 1998); Blake Altman, *Losing Letters: The Anti-Chirographic Turn in Canadian Bohemia* (Vancouver, BC: University of British Columbia Press, 2002).

66 Peter Lorre, "This Year's Assumption Graduates," *The Windsor Star*, June 20, 1954, A5. And yet, it is unclear whether or not Livingston ever competed in organized sports, including Canadian football.

67 Thomas Toogood, "Regarding the 'New Noise' in Folk Music Study," *The Blenheim News Tribune*, Dec 13, 1979, A2.

68 Fran Laney, *From Away: The Canadians Who Have Struggled South of the Border* (Montreal: McGill-Queen's University Press, 1990).

suggests that Livingston went rather to the northwestern shores of Newfoundland, where he lived for five years in relative solitude.[69]

It is at least clear that by 1967, now back in Toronto, Livingston had begun to present original work on what he termed "phonographic approaches to folkloristic methodology," having come to believe that the field-recording artist should (1) invariably wait until the informant has begun their song before pressing record, thus commencing the document *in medias res*; (2) anticipate the looming conclusion, through meditative listening, of the song in motion; (3) arrest the procedure before the song has ended, *musicorum interruptus*. [70] Further, it is certain that by 1972 at the latest, Livingston had begun to deploy this novel methodology through the collection of songs sung and perhaps also written by Canadian football players, though his method coupled with his archival practice—not writing anything down—has largely meant that the songs have been de facto signed as anonymous "folk" constructions. Finally, no one disputes that Livingston died in 1977 of heart failure in Trois-Pistoles, although I was unable to find any tributes or memorials in the major Canadian folklore journals.

Ergo, my growing infatuation with the CFL Sessions was directed to both sides of that delicate condenser microphone, propped between the folk song collector and his folk, carried from cavernous locker room to cavernous locker room across Canada in a dull green (or so I dreamed) duffel bag. Of course, there was the data: the words and tunes left as magnetic dust across those thick spools of tape. I was coming to sympathize with the sensitive singers Livingston had located, out of which he had squeezed such profound expressions and

---

69   Polk Halkman, *The Influence of Folk Tales and Ghost Stories of Newfoundland and Labrador* (Kentville, NS: Gaspereau Press, 1997).

70   There is only brief reference to one such talk in Grant Kennedy, *Folklore Scholarship as Folk Process* (Ottawa, ON: University of Ottawa Press, 1981). Livingston's three-point procedure, however, becomes very apparent as one listens to the hours upon hours of original tape that constitutes the CFL Sessions.

articulations, which now caressed my eardrums. The poetic starkness was like a screen pass to the soul.[71] Bodies could be blank slates, solidarity could be diagrammed with X's and O's, and teeth could be repaid with teeth in the cosmology of the CFL player. "Life *is* like Canadian football," I could not help but agree, wondering already about the political implications of the claim.

And yet, I was additionally pulled by Livingston himself. Here was a researcher who had abandoned any promise of reward, fame, or recompense; here was an artist who had abdicated even their own signature in the act of their final labours. Livingston's great refusal to write down anyone's name, including his own, his great refusal of commodities and credits and curriculum vitaes, should be inspiration to anyone interested in participating in the throbbing and the pulsing of real, human life. Is this not authenticity in the flesh, despite Dr. Bronnley's cynical doctrines? While eating my Vietnamese sandwiches, I wondered to what degree it was possible for me to follow Livingston in his move to acknowledge the irreducibly collaborative nature of creativity. Treating myself in the evenings with trips to the cinema or tavern, I pondered to what degree it might be possible for me also to become what I am.

In sum, this is what was going through my mind and belly as I listened to and edited down Livingston's hours of recordings, settling ultimately on those texts that best articulated the aesthetic *Weltanschauung* that I was slowly piecing together via the secondary literature. But also running through my mind (and belly), I must emphasize, was immense and over-

---

71 I am not the first to have experienced the sublime and even theological qualities of this classic offensive play, in which the quarterback drops, drawing the defensive line toward him, as though a decoy, only to sneak a short pass through to a nearby receiver with a fleet of blockers ready to go. See Mark Galli, "And God Created Football: Intimations of the Divine in a Well-Executed Screen Pass," ChristianityToday.com 28 (2010).

flowing joy, because it was by now obvious that, just as those dusty tapes had once served as channels for Livingston and his folk, I myself was learning to serve. My hands and voice were plugging into a generations-spanning system of folk song generation and transmission, which reverberated with the capacity to bring about cultural renewal and largescale socio-economic transformation.

As the reader of the present text reads and then rereads the songs contained within this volume, or better yet, embraces singing them, they have the opportunity to become part of this practical miracle as well. Together, we will haul in the most marvelous of Hail Mary passes. To echo the words of Staunton R. Livingston, "Those with ears, let them come here."[72]

---

[72] Staunton R. Livingston quoted in Dave Simpson, "Concert Review: A Tiresome Night for Folk Music," *The London Free Press*, June 23, 1969, A7.

ON DISCIPLINE

You're so pretty and you're so young.
I'll mess around a bit, but I can't come.
I need my legs and I need my energy.
If that's superstitious, then superstition is a part of me.

I wish I was an average guy;
I wish I was an average size;
But I'm a big strong man.
And I work to be big and strong; everyone does what
    they can.

I wish I could just play football
But in the off-season I work at the mall.[73]
I sell shoes.
If making money's a game, it's one I'll always lose.

---

73 Due to the modest average salary in the league, professional football players
in Canada have often needed to secure additional employment in the off-
season. This was especially true in the 1970s. Sandra Yokum, "For the Love of
the Game: Exploitation in Canadian Sport," *Canadian Journal of Labour* 120,
no. 3 (1993): 230–243.

I'm a bad lover and I can't dance
But you should see me down in a three-point stance.[74]
I'm a terrifying machine.
Know what I mean?

You're so pretty and you're so young.
I'll mess around a bit but I can't come.
I need my legs and I need my energy.
If that's superstitious, well, then superstition is a part of me.

---

74 An online branded football lesson, of all things, indicates the semiotic richness and functionality of a well-disciplined stance: "To set up in a good three-point stance, start with your feet shoulder-width apart, in line underneath your armpits. Get in an athletic stance by sinking your tail and bending your knees. From there, if you are on the right-hand side of the offensive line, put your right foot back to roughly a heel-to-toe relationship, so that your feet are staggered. Then, lean forward and put your right hand down to the ground. Keep your head up and back flat. If there is too much weight on your hands, you could fall face first. [...] When you become confident and comfortable in your three-point stance, not only will you have personal success but you'll also create success for your team." Dick's Pro Tips, *Dick's Sporting Goods*, January 2, 2021.

LINEBACKER PASSING THROUGH[75]

We were higher than the territories,
Put your hands together for me;
I'll never feel like that again
And I hadn't before.

We ran hard like two muddy rivers
And then fell on our backs, you called it "practice";
It was quick and painful,
Like February in the mountains.

When your clothes are dry, you're going away.
When your clothes are dry, buddy, you're going away.
I said your clothes are dry, so go away.
We closed our eyes and believed in the rain.

---

75 In Canadian football, as in American football, the linebacker is positioned behind the line of scrimmage; they generally are required to read or interpret the offensive play, whether run or pass, and to adjust their position accordingly: on running plays they move forward, whereas on passing plays they drop backwards, covering receivers according to either zone or man-to-man schemas. However, it is also the linebacker who is often responsible for blitzing—in which case they do not need to interpret the offensive play at all, just to launch themselves through a particular gap. When successful, this tactic is very pleasurable for an audience to behold. Nick Trujillo, "Machines, Missiles, and Men: Images of the Male Body on ABC's *Monday Night Football*," *Sociology of Sport Journal* 12, no. 4 (1995): 403–423.

MADONNA WITH NO DIVINITY

by Jeseka Hickey[76]

What do I do with the feelings I feel?
With the wounds that I dress, so the wounds they can heal?
How do I take these feelings away,
To help their minds rest, to live in their play?
But is it a game on the battlefield?

Everybody's praying for a touchdown.
I score touchdowns.
They are praying to me:
The Madonna with no divinity.

What can I do for these broken-down homes,
For these beaten-up bodies built with now worn-out bones.
I can take these hands, these healing hands
And touch down their bodies like it was the land,
And trick them to think that the strength is their own.

Everybody's praying for a touchdown.
I score touchdowns.
They are praying to me:
The Madonna with no divinity.[77]

---

76 I have often been asked which CFL players wrote and sang which songs, but,
given Livingston's sonographic approach to fieldwork, this knowledge is lost.
I claim that to wonder is to miss the point profoundly. However, authorship of
"Madonna with No Divinity" has been verified because upon public release of
The CFL Sessions, former trainer Jeseka Hickey wrote me an email, the details
of which have subsequently undergone verification. I include her name at her
insistence, if not her version of the title.

77 Not necessarily profane, however, as one cannot help but be reminded of
the "Epicurean matrix of matter without form, of tiny molecules stringing
and swilling with love and danger and time," of which Livingston spoke at
great lengths in his first slam poetry performance. Staunton R. Livingston
quoted in Darleen Pageant, "Local Poets Mix It Up—and Mash," *Toronto Star*,
July 1967, A12.

"E" IS FOR END ZONE[78]

I've crossed my share of lines
And screwed my share of women.
I'm not steady
But don't you call my crooked.
I haven't told a lie since my dad died.

I've wiped some blood from my hands
But I've never needed any bandages.
I've been called names
But never "chicken."
I've been fighting since my dad died.[79]

But you know I've held and shook some hands.
Some people love me and some people hate me.
Sometimes I forget why I decided to live this life
    of mine alone.
But I remember after, when I masturbate.
I've been running all my life.

---

78 Livingston's recording of "'E' for End Zone" is one of the few on which his method seems to disappear or falter. Before the music begins, one can hear a chair scratch across the floor and then the performer, I believe, taps the microphone before stating, "This song is called '"E" for End Zone.'" Therefore, this is the only song in the CFL Sessions whose title is certain. The other titles having been hypothesized by the present author.

79 Due to his imposing size, one cannot help but wonder about the nature of Livingston's relationship to brutality and sadism. One additionally wonders whether, during this famously informal period in CFL history, Livingston ever got to see the field himself, even the practice field. On the fluidity of the identity of the average team roster in the CFL in the 1970s, see, for example, Stan Plempton, *Once We Were Kings: My Life in Football in Canada* (Toronto, ON: Cormorant Books, 1987).

part two

SONGS OF THE FIELD

TROUBLED IN MIND

What is the meaning of communication? Countless competing answers have been offered since the game-changing moment—whenever this game-changing moment might have occurred—at which human beings first began to reflect upon and articulate ideas about the species-wide propensity to divulge or convey information.[1]

According to the cyberneticist luminaries Claude Shannon and Warren Weaver, whose 1949 collaborative book has proven astonishingly durable, communication is both "the procedures by which one mind may affect another" and "the procedures by means of which one mechanism (say automatic equipment to track an airplane, and to compute its probable future positions) affects another mechanism (say, a guided missile chasing this airplane)."[2] To put this another way, the act of communication is a straight shot—akin to a bomb or tailback headed straight up the middle—the fundamental problem of which is that all possible channels carry alongside their messages, necessarily, a certain amount of noise.[3]

---

1   By definition, there is no recorded trace of this presumably prehistoric moment. However, for a highly original analysis of more recent developments in the history of the concept, such as can be found in the work of Plato and Jesus, see John Durham Peters, *Speaking into the Air: A History of the Idea of Communication* (Chicago, IL: University of Chicago Press, 1999).

2   Warren Weaver, "Recent Contributions to the Mathematical Theory of Communication," in Claude Shannon and Warren Weaver, *The Mathematical Theory of Communication* (Urbana, IL: University of Illinois Press, 1949), 3. Although Weaver merely wrote an introductory essay, which was placed before Shannon's pioneering research, the text as a whole is often referred to as the Shannon-Weaver theory of communication.

3   Claude E. Shannon, "The Mathematical Theory of Communication," in Claude E. Shannon and Warren Weaver, *The Mathematical Theory of Communication* (Urbana, IL: University of Illinois Press, 1949), 29–115.

And how to distinguish signal (i.e., payload) from noise (i.e., disturbance)? How can anyone, in any situation, be sure the message sent ever exactly arrives? That the encoded symbols signify that which they were intended to signify? These are ancient problems plaguing numerous domains, from military coordination to long-distance romantic relationships to, yes, folk song collection. Luckily for Shannon and Weaver, however, and luckily too for the behemoth telecom corporations continuing to exploit their pioneering research, not to mention the reader of the present text, the issue of noise turns out to be solvable via mathematical theorems that utilize the principle of redundancy.[4]

Be that as it may, there have been numerous attempts to revise or outright reject the Shannon-Weaver model with respect to *human* communication. For example, James Carey has explored the colonialist roots of transmission-oriented inflections of the concept, suggesting we reconsider the term's originary community-building and social—one might even add *folkloristic*—connotations.[5] Shannon and Weaver are implied but not named in this critique. Similarly, Stuart Hall has identified in the case of television broadcasting a myriad of possible "decoding" positions.[6] Recall that for Shannon and Weaver, the receiver was only a sitting duck, waiting to be blasted by a belligerence of messages, possessing neither weapons nor armour of its own. But in Hall's theory, receivers are active agents able to reassemble the contents of any communicational event vis-à-vis the intentions, so often nefarious, of sovereign transmitters. Neither sitting ducks

---

4   Claude E. Shannon and Warren Weaver, *The Mathematical Theory of Communication* (Urbana, IL: University of Illinois Press, 1949).

5   James Carey, *Communication as Culture: Essays on Media and Society* (New York, NY: Routledge, 2008).

6   Stuart Hall, "Encoding/Decoding" in *Media and Cultural Keywords, Second Edition*, eds. Meenakshi Gigi Durham and Douglas M. Kellner, 137–144 (Malden, MA: Wiley-Blackwell, 2012).

nor dupes, receivers are instead guerilla warriors in Hall's agile model.[7]

I was thinking about these debates and, of course, about Staunton R. Livingston, as September transitioned to October and the leaves turned bright crimson and orange—I was back in London, my Forest City. Was it possible that Livingston could find a posthumous shelter in the discipline of communication studies, despite having already been hostilely rejected within the field of folklore?[8] If so, was communication for Livingston an act of transmission or an act of ritual? Or was it something else entirely? I pondered these and other questions, marching in the morning along the river to my cubbyhole office on the ninth floor of the library, crawling and backstroking during noontime lane swim, and finally returning to my underground home led by the light of the stars, finishing the day with a steaming bowl of beans and rice, or some other modest yet nourishing substance that was also not too difficult to chew.

Of course, my own methodological dilemma—how to piece together historical information when textual records

---

7   Hall thus anticipates the digital tactical media movement, which explores the power of individuals to creatively resists cultural structures of power. See, for example, Critical Art Ensemble, *The Electronic Disturbance* (Brooklyn, NY: Autonomedia, 1994); Nick Dyer-Witheford and Greig de Peuter, *Games of Empire: Global Capitalism and Video Games* (Minneapolis, MN: University of Minnesota Press, 2009), 185–214; David Garcia and Geert Lovink, "The ABC of Tactical Media" (post to Nettime mailing list, 1997); Rita Raley, *Tactical Media* (Minneapolis, MN: University of Minnesota Press, 2009).

8   See Dale Ricks, "Song Collecting Is Song Collecting," *Canadian Folkloristics Bulletin* 42, no. 1 (2004): 35. Ricks' critique, albeit brief and buried in a footnote, is twofold. First, he claims that, by cutting off the ends and the beginnings of songs, an archivist such as Livingston can only misinform and thus deprive "future generations." Second, he argues that Livingston's refusal to write down the names of the performers he recorded is a sign that he was planning to exploit their creative labour like so many other folklorists and song collectors of previous generations, a plan cut short, however, by his untimely death in Trois-Pistoles. I argue that these claims tell us more about the poverty of imagination within contemporary Canadian folklore scholarship than they tell us about anything else.

were so obviously lacking—would first need to be solved since, again, Staunton R. Livingston had not maintained any chirographic documentary practice. This problem did not discourage me, however. I envisioned myself as a lead blocker or horseman, clearing the path for Livingston's delicate, invisible motions, motivated as I was by the universality of entropy and the inherent corruptibility of all things.[9]

---

9 "We have already seen that certain organisms, such as man [sic], tend for a time to maintain and often even to increase the level of their organization, as a local enclave in the general stream of increasing entropy, of increasing chaos and de-differentiation. Life is an island here and now in a dying world. The process by which we living beings resist the general stream of corruption and decay is known as *homeostasis.*" Norbert Wiener, *The Human Use of Human Beings* (London, UK: Free Association Books, 1989), 92. This does not mean, however, that folk song collection is a homeostatic process; in fact, contra Wiener, I argue that there is no room for the veneration of homeostasis in Livingstonian theory.

DOWN BY YOUR SHADY HARBOUR
from Okie Langlois[10]
Recorded in Dartmouth, Nova Scotia

That night was cool, when you left for school;
I could tell the year would be long
With you so far, across, away,
And me with just your song,
Me with just your song.

You read books over there, and learn over there,
As I walk about the shoreline.
The last place you touched here means so much, dear,[11]
Your sacred place till the morning,
Our sacred place till the morning.

Your thick dark hair, it seems just there
Hovering o'er the horizon.
I breathe you in, I think of sins
And go back to work in the morning.
I go back to work in the morning.

---

10   I captured this version of "Down by Your Shady Harbour" in Dartmouth by the water after gormandizing a milky Maritime donair wrap. The noises emanating from my gastrointestinal system nearly drowned out the performance; luckily, I was able to extract the words nonetheless at the transcription stage. Let this stand as a vicarious lesson for future folk song collectors: Eat neither meat nor dairy directly before a field encounter, if at all.

11   A clear expression of sympathetic magic, whereby distinct objects and entities are able to maintain a kind of causal relationship, by virtue of having once been in contact. James George Frazer, *The Golden Bough* (London: Macmillan, 1963). For a post-structuralist spin by which I have been influenced, see also Michael Taussig, *Mimesis and Alterity* (New York: Routledge, 1993), 47–51.

Girls here mock me, they don't stop;
They mock, they mock me daily.
They say you won't be faithful to me,
But I don't pay them mind, dear.
I wait down by the harbour,
Down by your shady harbour.

AM I BORN TO DIE?

It was late November when I first mentioned Staunton R. Livingston to Dr. Bronnley at the wine bar in downtown London. We met before his train trip that evening back to Toronto, the most immediate purpose of which was that his signature was required on that semester's progress report. Was I making "excellent" progress, "good" progress, or merely "satisfactory" progress? These bureaucratic rituals are the products of madness, but Bronnley had marked "excellent" each term thus far, additionally imprinting strongly enthusiastic if brief comments into the text boxes. This was important because funding in the doctoral program was contingent on these otherwise meaningless documents.[12] "Promising work in development!" he had last written. "Excellent!!" he scribbled this time, redundantly.

Our chat that night was both productive and stressful, as was by now customary. Dr. Bronnley was generous with his time, generally wanting to meet every two weeks or so, yet he often made me wary of my *self*, especially the degree to which I had yet listened to or read things that I should have, by now, already listened to or read. "Really, you don't know Spandau Ballet?" he once asked, brows high and furrowed. "The word 'few' is only used in reference to countable nouns," he also instructed with a sigh. Hot shame engulfed me in these moments, impelling note taking and follow-up questioning. So, by our second round that night, I had sketched a list of items to procure from the library, this time on the topics of civility, reverberation, and the Renaissance

---

12 Preposterously, one needed to maintain "good" and not "satisfactory" progress in the program in order to guarantee funding. See the University of Western Ontario Communication Studies Program, "Program Expectations and Regulations," 2008.

carnival in addition to the top two all-time films involving disco.[13]

Of course, it was not always obvious *how* Bronnley's suggestions related to my dissertation topic, but this was apparently part of the contest. A map of trials and tribulations was bestowed, ancient and modern recipes of potential potions or spells lent, and the student charged with connecting the gifts and assembling therewith new, useful knowledge. The hero's quest, in essence—and thus graduate school earning its place as merely another genre of folk song.[14]

While we waited in the barrel-lined cellar for the cheque, Dr. Bronnley offered congratulations regarding the accumulating press for the *The CFL Sessions*, a volume of which I had recently released online. The *Globe and Mail*, the *Toronto Star*, and CBC Radio had run features in the past month; these were noted in a departmental bulletin.[15] He thought that I should be sure to list these media appearances on my CV: "This will be good for the Social Sciences and Humanities Research Council scholarship application," he said, scribbling his signature and glancing over, one last time, at our waitress's bottom while she sauntered back to the bar. Since the topic had naturally arisen, this appeared to be an opportune moment to introduce the topic of Staunton R. Livingston, which would need to be done

13 Dir. John Badham, *Saturday Night Fever* (London, UK: Robert Stigwood Organization, 1977); Peter Doyle, *Echo and Reverb: Fabricating Space in Popular Music Recording, 1900–1960* (Middletown, CT: Wesleyan University Press, 1997); Dir. Robert Klane, *Thank God It's Friday* (Los Angeles, CA: Motown Productions, 1978); Richard Sennett, *The Fall of Public Man* (New York, NY: WW Norton, 1974); Peter Stallybrass and Allon White, *The Politics & Poetics of Transgression* (Ithaca, NY: Cornell University Press, 1986).

14 See, especially, function XI of Propp's Morphology: "The Hero Leaves Home." Vladimir Propp, *Morphology of the Folk Tale*, trans. Laurence Scott (Austin, TX: University of Texas Press, 1968), 39.

15 Henry Adam Svec, *The CFL Sessions*, http://www.thecflsessions.ca. For an example of the coverage, see Chris Zelkovich, "Football Folk's a Passing Fancy," *Toronto Star*, August 9, 2009.

tactfully, knowing what I did about human psychology in the field of communication.[16]

Certain details of the pitch remain foggy. "You would not believe the backstory here, Dr. Bronnley," I likely began. I may have blubbered about Livingston's position on the margins of academia and his sexy biography, beginning in Windsor and ending with his mysterious death in Quebec. There is a good chance that I additionally divulged Livingston's understanding of sound as overflowing, immanent plenitude, as revolutionary substance in and of itself, my theory of which had already begun to percolate. For this was obviously the core of the project. "Sound has a magical, you could say *de-territorializing*, like, potency, for Staunton R. Livingston," I might have said.[17]

However, buzzed both by my newfound love for Canadian folk song collection and by the beer—it was a relief to discover that the wine bar sold Labatt products—I definitely hinted that the work of Staunton R. Livingston might be the new focus of my dissertation project. "I see this as an opportunity, Professor. I want my constructions to similarly intervene in the becoming of materiality."

Dr. Bronnley's response was a durational spell of silence, brow wrinkled and eyes narrowing. What could I do but wait—for some signal of interest or encouragement, the candle on our table casting flickering, ancient light? Yet, I received no such signal. "Folklorists," he abruptly guffawed, then donned his scarf and fedora. I followed Dr. Bronnley out

---

16 Of particular relevance is the social judgment theory developed by Muzafer Sherif, which claims that persuasion has less to do with the rationality of an argument and more to do with the apparent relationship between that argument and the audience's preconceived range of acceptable positions, in which "ego-involvement" plays a determining role. Muzafer Sherif and Carl Hovland, *Social Judgment: Assimilation and Contrast Effects in Communication and Attitude Change* (New Haven, CT: Yale University, 1961).

17 Gilles Deleuze and Félix Guattari, *A Thousand Plateaus: Capitalism and Schizophrenia*, trans. Brian Massumi (Minneapolis, MN: University of Minnesota Press, 1987).

onto Talbot Street and he exclaimed, as though to himself, his love for Fleet Foxes before he finally fled in the direction of the railway lines.[18]

Whether by accident or otherwise, had I not recovered from the dustbin of history an object of value? I was certain that this was so. Why could the gatekeepers of academia not recognize me as a game-ready rookie?

From kindergarten on, I had been what one would call a teachable student. Eager to scale the ivory tower, I often supplicated myself by the founts of knowledge to which I had had access. Was I by now enlightened? Was this what it meant to have been enlightened?[19] For what I decided on my journey home to the Institute's basement that night—the first snowflakes of the semester softly beginning to fall, enveloping the Forest City in a sound-cancelling blanket, my Wrangler jean hems dragging through the fresh, cold crystals—was that if the term "folklorist" could elicit such-like cackling from Dr. Bronnley, then a folklorist was exactly what I was going to become.

---

18 Fleet Foxes, *Fleet Foxes* (Seattle, WT: Sub Pop, 2008).

19 See Immanuel Kant, *An Answer to the Question: What is Enlightenment?* (London, UK: Penguin, 2009).

THAT OLD-TIME MOUNTAIN DEW[20]

from Brigid Bunyan
Recorded in Sarnia, Ontario[21]

That old-time mountain dew
Will make a singer out of you,
Make a real man out of you,
Old-time mountain dew.[22]

You can lay about the grasses,
Make advances and make passes
At all the bonnie lasses
Who cross your sunny way.

Ask them where they're going,
Or if they wanna be a rose in
The weedy life
Of a good drunk Christian man.

That old-time mountain dew
Will make a singer out of you,
Make a real man out of you,
Old-time mountain dew.

---

20 "That Old-Time Mountain Dew" derives in ethics and tone, if not in melody or poëtics, from the Irish folk song "The Rare Old Mountain Dew." The song has undergone deep and fascinating alterations as it has moved to North America by way of Appalachia, finally settling in numerous regions across Canada, yet still in motion. See Annette Hempel, *Drinking Songs of North America* (Jackson, MS: University of Mississippi Press, 1999).

21 My trusty Shure SM58 held solidly by her mouth, Brigid Bunyan stood and sang as she gazed across the water at the United States of America, full of longing and desire. And, as I held the microphone, so did I.

22 This song is *not* about the PepsiCo-produced soda pop Mountain Dew®. "Mountain dew" is an Irish euphemism for moonshine, which, however, has not stopped PepsiCo from exploiting "The Rare Old Mountain Dew" in their marketing campaigns. See Michelle Dean, "Here Comes the Hillbilly, Again: What *Honey Boo Boo* Really Says About American Culture," *Slate* (August 24, 2012): n.p.

BOUND FOR GLORY

There is a baffling contradiction at the core of modern folkloristic practice. The object of the quest has so often been framed as a relic—as medium by which a version of the past can be retrieved. The corresponding type of folklorist has consequently, or perhaps causally, been presented as possessing a nostalgic or conservative disposition; this folklorist gardens in neo-Medieval fashion.[23] Conversely, one of the key implements in the toolbox of countless folk fieldworkers is the automobile, that glistening and high-octane symbol of speed, progress, and American individualism.[24]

I would like the reader of the present text to visualize this paradoxical conundrum. The modern folklorist moves toward an imagined collectivist past, eager to locate organic as opposed to mass-produced cultural remnants, and does so by blazing down the highway in the most mechanical of solipsistic consumer contraptions, the Model T or, more recently, the Tesla.[25]

---

23   Ian McKay, *The Quest of the Folk* (Montreal, QC: McGill-Queen's University Press, 1994).

24   On the cultural contradictions of folk song collection, see Robert Cantwell, *When We Were Good: The Folk Revival* (Cambridge, MA: Harvard University Press, 1993); Benjamin Filene, *Romancing the Folk: Public Memory and American Roots Music* (Chapel Hill, NC: University of North Carolina Press, 2000); Marybeth Hamilton, *In Search of the Blues: Black Voices, White Visions* (New York, NY: Basic Books, 1998); LeRoi Jones, *Blues People: Negro Music in White America* (New York, NY: W. Morrow, 1963); Karl Hagstrom Miller, *Segregating Sound: Inventing Folk and Pop Music in the Age of Jim Crow* (Durham, NC: Duke University Press, 2010).

25   As a cultural-material artifact, the Tesla automobile articulates entanglements endemic to the Canadian folklore scene; it is thus no surprise that the car has seemed to be popular among the professional Canadian song-collecting set. The Tesla is both an object with magical powers capable of rectifying the despoliation effects of modernity and the perpetuation of the core causes of those very despoliation effects (the logic of capital). Cf. Karl Marx, *The Poverty of Philosophy* (Moscow: Co-operative Publishing Society of Foreign Workers in the U.S.S.R., 1935).

Be that as it may, during my most active period of collecting I did not own an automobile. If I had designs to record a woodsman in Peterborough, Ontario, I did not only need to travel to Peterborough, I had to take at least two or perhaps three different Greyhound busses.[26] I waited, usually three, but as many as five, hours at the bus station in downtown Toronto, reading my books and making my preparatory notes, knapsack carefully guarded on a neighbouring seat. Even without errors, the journey required at minimum one full day—from dawn until midnight—before I was snugly back home in the basement of the Institute. As you can imagine, there are, of course, many possible setbacks lying in wait for the Canadian folk song collector.

I first began to conduct my own field recordings within London's city limits. After a year or two of graduate school, as word of my presence in the Forest City spread, every other weekend there seemed to be a touring band or singer-songwriter playing in town who would almost always ask, in the days leading up to the show, whether or not I had a place for them to sleep.[27] I do not enjoy entertaining, but I appreciated these events for their power to suspend my regular routine; it was rejuvenating to witness performers committing to the delivery of musical compositions regardless of their audience's size or interest level. My earliest field recordings were thus made in the mornings after these nights out, before my depleted guests got back into their van and continued down the road. I began by asking whether they knew any folk songs, which they almost always did. Sometimes they even tried to teach me how to sing or play a song or two.

It is important to note that, at this point, it was not yet clear to me how my efforts as a real, live folk song collector

---

26 There were, and there are, no passenger trains to Peterborough.

27 These travelling musicians tended to take for granted, therefore, the gift-economy principles that ground their folk-musical communities. See Marcel Mauss, *The Gift: The Form and Reason for Exchange in Archaic Societies*, trans. W. D. Halls (London, UK: Routledge, 1990).

related to my emerging scholarly research on Livingston. The gradual accumulation of sound recordings made via microphone and cassette recorder felt formally disjointed from my usual gradual accumulation of ideas via pencils and pens. This discernment perhaps had to do with the varying natures of these distinct forms of labour, the former involving the rolling up of one's sleeves for embodied, face-to-face engagement of fellow creatures, the latter involving the wearing of high-strength reading glasses and the insertion of industrial earplugs.[28] The absurd and nihilistic values of the neoliberal university—already deeply infusing both my neurons and musculature—likely also played a role in my inability, in those days, to synthesize theory with praxis.

---

28   Another way of describing this liminality is that I was stuck between two distinct historical "discourse networks," which have been defined by Friedrich Kittler as "the network of technologies and institutions that allow a given culture to select, store, and process relevant data." Friedrich Kittler, *Discourse Networks, 1800/1900*, trans. Michael Metteer (Stanford, CA: Stanford University Press, 1990), 369.

PAY DAY

My inner conflict between professional scholar and amateur folklorist was deferred, if not fundamentally resolved, by my discovery of the arts and culture granting systems in Canada.[29] Although there were not any clearly designated folklore programs circa 2010, I achieved victory on my first attempt through the Ontario Arts Council's Integrated Arts program. Their mandate was to support projects combining multiple disciplines, such that the boundaries between these disciplines were thereby transgressed in the work, and, additionally, to support projects involving clowns.[30] I was ecstatic when awarded $11,000 CAD on the merits of a proposal boasting the complete documentation of the totality of Canadian folk song, having argued in my application that folk song itself—essentially, *necessarily*—transgresses all disciplinary boundaries, and sometimes may involve clowns (the latter claim admittedly a cynical bluff). But please do not hate the player, dear reader of the present text. Hate solely the game, as Karl Marx was perhaps the first to urge.[31]

On the point of critique, the occurrence of granting allows for the empirical investigation of a crucial question: Does either the capitalistic wage- or the bureaucratic salary-relation

---

29 Amateur is meant not in the pejorative sense but as "[o]ne who loves or is fond of; one who has a taste for anything." *Oxford English Dictionary* (Oxford, UK: Oxford University Press, 2020).

30 This category was not to be confused with a separate one, the Multidisciplinary Arts program, mandated to support projects combining multiple disciplines, such that the boundaries between these disciplines were maintained in the work, and, additionally not to support projects involving clowns.

31 Karl Marx, *Capital: A Critique of Political Economy*, translated by Ben Fowkes (New York, NY: Vintage Books, 1977).

fundamentally alter the work of the folk song collector?[32] In my case, I maintain that the Ontario Arts Council grant enabled the *amplification* or *extension* of activities already underway without fundamentally altering their character. I was able to email all discernible nodes in my musical network—emails sent, naturally, from a brand-new Apple laptop computer—and thereby to retrieve the locations and contact information of dozens of possible informants. After conducting the first round of auditions by telephone, I travelled on weekends and holidays to cities and towns across the country, encoding voices and tunes into, first, my new digital device's hard-disk drive and, second, over onto my trusty new external hard drive.[33] Furthermore, I was able to entice potential singers with artist fees, perhaps the most significant amplification of all. My going rate was $100 CAD per song, a not-inconsiderable sum for only a few minutes of work, though on occasion I offered more or less, depending on the situation.[34]

Therefore, as my secondary practice (folk song collection) ballooned to occupy space roughly equal in volume to my primary practice (scholarly research on the topic of folk song collection *qua* communication), I postulated new relationships between the two sets of endeavours, an unavoidable step. Was it not possible that the *doing* of folk song collection was, in its own way, a form of research in the field of communication

---

32 In posing this question I am following the lead of the Frankfurt School. See, for example, my boys Max Horkheimer and Theodor Adorno, *The Dialectic of Enlightenment*, trans. Edmund Jephcott (Stanford, CA: Stanford University Press, 1972).

33 The last things an industrious folk song collector desires are any data corruption issues. Geoffrey Lidell, "Information Management in the Folkloristic Context," *Song Collector Magazine* 476, no. 190 (2010): 27–28.

34 This admission may compromise my ability to coax songs from future reluctant folksingers without blowing immediately my budget, but I will honestly state that the most I have paid for a single performance is $700. Thankfully, however, the overabundant generosity of the majority of the folk has outweighed the stingier minority.

theory?[35] For example: accepting a home-cooked meal in a quaint cottage in Summerside, or encountering a pack of majestic coyotes on Grand Manan? Participating in a small orgy in a living room in Arnprior, or accepting a ride back to the GTA from a hopped-up transport truck driver at a North Bay Esso? What about bleeding from the head and hands as I stumbled through Toronto's streets, having been kettled by the militarized police thugs ordered to repress democratic, anti-corporate dissent during the G20 Summit, in which I found myself accidentally entangled while on layover? Artificial lines, like those once etched in sand to demarcate the first cities carved from the surrounding wilds, may once have been required, but the phony boundaries demanded to divide my primary passions were becoming obsolete, in my view.[36]

I must insist above all that Dr. Bronnley's description to the appeal committee, of my *alleged* failures as evidence of "indolence," is inaccurate. Neither my will nor my commitment to scholarly inquiry flagged as result of my frequent field-recording trips to Saint John's, Dartmouth, Ottawa, Sarnia, Winnipeg, Regina, and the countryside and backroads between. I was generating knowledge the whole time.[37] There are many pejorative terms that can fairly and reasonably be applied to my person and conduct, but, as is demonstrated by the present volume, even just by the next several pages, lazy is not one of them.

---

35 Within communication studies, if not adjacent fields such as visual art, I was frankly ahead of my time in asking this question. On theory/praxis combinations in visual art, see Natalie S. Loveless, "Practice in the Flesh of Theory: Art, Research and the Fine Arts PhD," *Canadian Journal of Communication* 37, no. 1 (2012): 93–108.

36 Hazel Honour, *Writing the World* (Toronto, ON: University of Toronto Press, 1987).

37 Paolo Virno, *A Grammar of the Multitude: For an Analysis of Contemporary Forms of Life*, trans. Isabella Bertoletti, James Cascaito, Andre Casson (Los Angeles, CA: Semiotext(e), 2004).

SAVE YOUR MONEY WHILE YOU'RE YOUNG
from Laura Barrett[38]
Recorded in Toronto, Ontario

Save your money while you're young,
While you think you're having fun
With all the girls you never met before.
Don't you know that all your hard-earned dough
Will surely go...

So much faster than you think.
And that second second drink
Finds you underneath the table,
When you've forgotten every dollar from today
Could've lived another way.

Baby, you keep your eye on the bottom line,
Say we save up enough to buy ourselves some time
With no money at all.

You could spread your cash around,
Sow those pennies in the ground.
Let's get it down on paper first;
Because it's guaranteed to increase
If we buy into it, at least.

---

38 There are many different ways to capture sound electrically or electronically, and the flexible folk song collector requires an expansive arsenal of tools, including condenser microphones, shotgun microphones, stereo condenser microphones, and even contact microphones. Kay Kaufman Shelemay, "Recording Technology and Ethnomusicological Scholarship," in *Comparative Musicology and Anthropology of Music: Essays on the History of Ethnomusicology*, eds. B. Nettl and P. Bohlman (Chicago, IL: University of Chicago Press, 1991), 277–292. However, in the case of the legendary folksinger Laura Barrett, she simply emailed me her recording.

WHEN THE ICE WORMS NEST AGAIN

from Jenny Mitchell
Recorded in Guelph, Ontario

Go out after dawn and they'll be gone.
Soon even night will be too warm.
When the ice that they love starts to fade,
They won't find the frost they need,
They won't know the night from day.
Lately our cold just isn't so cold.

Back in 1887, the ice worms were in heaven,[39]
On the glaciers of Washington, Alaska and BC and Oregon,
You'd look and they'd be seven million strong.
Just hiding in the dark, in the ice where they belong.
How do the ice worms tunnel?
Do they melt the ice with chemicals they secrete?
How do the ice worms tunnel?
Is it through microscopic fissures in ice sheets?

It might be cold,
But one day I hope for them
To find a cold that's cold enough for them to nest again.
I hope the ice worms nest again.

---

39 Scientists know little about the marvelous ice worm. It is unique in the animal kingdom for its ability to derive energy from the cold, which astoundingly violates the second law of thermodynamics. See Michael J. Napolitano and Daniel H. Shain, "Four Kingdoms on Glacier Ice: Convergent Energetic Processes Boost Energy Levels as Temperatures Fall," *Proceedings of the Royal Society of London Series B: Biological Sciences* 271, no. 5 (2004): S273–S276. Mitchell's concise lament, which clearly describes the organism but also points to numerous possible technological applications, demonstrates the rich potential of folk song as a medium of techno-scientific knowledge production.

NELLIE[40]

from Mathias Kom
Recorded in Saint John's, Newfoundland[41]

Oh, pretty little Nellie, she's coming o'er the hill,
Filled with charming kindness and the goodest of good will.
I asked her, "Nellie, where you coming from?"
    And she said: "Friend,
I'm after coming from the wake of my true love, for he
    is dead."

Well, Nellie, she was lovely, though a tear was in her eye.
She stumbled with her heavy purse and I could not
    stand by.
I said, "Nellie, love, please let me take your handbag
    for you dear."
And she said: "In my time of need, I'm glad to
    find a kind man here."

So, I took Nellie's purse off Nellie and, "Oh Nellie, dear,"
    I cried,
"This handbag's mighty heavy, what do you have inside?"
But she just laughed and told me: "Mind the wax
    of your own bees.
I'm a-grievin' for my true love and your question's
    vexing me."

---

40 The standing of femme fatale "Nellie" has varied greatly throughout the history of Canadian folk song scholarship. Kom's variation is wholly unique, in my view. See, for example, Fran Gamble, *Nellie the Nomad* (Waterloo, ON: Wilfred Laurier University Press, 1991); Raymond Horbinek, *Murder and Blood in the Music and Tales of Regular People* (Calgary, AB: University of Calgary Press, 1982); Peter Warner, *Canadian Folk Legends and Heroes* (Winnipeg, MB: ARP Books, 2010); Bertie Zork, "Reconsidering Nellie," *Mosaic* 22, no. 2 (1989): 230–247.

41 I recorded Mathias with his merry band of Newfoundlanders on a rocky cliff overlooking the Atlantic Ocean. I later learned that, no mere vagabond, Mathias Kom was in fact studying toward his PhD degree in ethnomusicology. Mathias Kom, "Cosmopolitan Intimacy: Antifolk in Berlin and New York." PhD diss., Memorial University of Newfoundland, 2017.

Well, on we went down past the tracks and past the
    grocery store,
And Nellie's bag was heavy and I could not wait no more.
So I took the smallest peak inside, and Lord what did I find?
The head of Nellie's own true love; his eyes were staring
    back at mine.

Like a little girl I screamed and dropped the bag
    unto the ground.
The parking lot was empty, there was no one else around.
Fair Nellie, well, she laughed and said: "I know you
    think it's queer,
But I went to the wake of my own true love and
    this is my souvenir."

She said: "I thank you for your chivalry and generosity,
But it's a pity that you have such cat-like curiosity."
Then fast she flashed a knife and passed a bloody
    swish and blur.
She said: "Farewell my own true love." These were the last
    words that I heard.

Well, who's that girl with such sadness in her eyes?
She walks with such a mournful step, such a heavy
    purse besides.
Oh, beware, my helpful gentlemen, be wary of my mistake,
For it's pretty little Nellie coming home from the wake.
Yes, it's pretty little Nellie coming home from my own wake.

MAGGIE HOWIE[42]

from Olenka Krakus
Recorded in London, Ontario

Maggie Howie, what a girl.
Lost her way in this cruel, cruel world.
It happened when I was almost ten:
We watched her sink into drink and men.
And when we heard, we were saddened and stirred.

Father John was an honest man,
He raised his daughter and worked his land.
But when the rain washed his crop away,
He didn't last near a month and day.
And when he died, Maggie cried and cried.

And then the men started coming round,
Bringing whisky and evening gowns.
And Maggie danced and Maggie swayed,
Maggie drank all her blues away.
And when she smiled, it was reckless and wild.

One evening when I was walking home,
I came upon her, afraid and alone.
An angry lover had hit her hard,
She had fled through a neighbour's yard.
And I held her hand, and we hid from that man.

---

42 Mainstream versions of the ballad of Maggie Howie had already been collected by Newbell Niles Puckett and Edith Fowke by the time I put my Shure SM58 microphone in front of Olenka Krakus in a Richmond Street loft apartment on one muggy, Southwestern Ontario summer night. One striking difference is that Krakus's version focalizes the action through a bystander or friend, rather than the murderer, thereby offering much more detail than is generally found in variations of the song regarding the tragic folk hero's short life. Cf. Edith Fowke, ed., *Folk Songs of Ontario* (New York, NY: Folkways, 1958).

But in the morning I woke alone,
So I sleepily headed home.
But then the constable came around.
And told us Maggie Howie drowned,
And when I heard, I shook at every word.
I cried and cried, 'cause no one really tried.

HOW WE GOT BACK TO THE WOODS THIS YEAR[43]

from Andrew Vincent
Recorded in Lindsay, Ontario

And the woods are filled with rockers[44]
With heavy hearts and empty coffers.
Hey man, I've got an idea,
How we can get back to the woods this year.

'Cause these club gigs break my heart.
And the suburbs don't get my art.
Hey, mom, I've got an idea,
You said you weren't going to the lake this year.

I packed my bags and turned out the light.
I've got a map, and dad's advice.

All I need are trees and air.
When it gets cold, people get scared.
So hey, man, you can bring up the drums,
And we'll rock these woods till the maples run.

Quit your job and skip the rent.
This record won't cost a cent.

---

43   The woods in question are, according to my informant via discussion after his performance, in Muskoka. I encountered Vincent in a cottage town in the Kawarthas, however, and we had a fun night together.

44   Your average Canadian folklorist (e.g., Dale Ricks) would likely have passed over this song due to the connection in both form and content to rock music—Andrew additionally played an electric guitar—despite the fact that there is a long tradition of radical song collectors taking seriously the folkloristic function and generic features of rock 'n' roll musics. Alan Lomax, for instance, programmed the group The Cadillacs alongside Pete Seeger, Muddy Waters, and Jimmy Driftwood in his controversial Folksong '59 concert at Carnegie Hall, long before Bob Dylan even considered plugging in his Stratocaster. Ronald D. Cohen, *Rainbow Quest: The Folk Music Revival and American Society, 1940–1970* (Amherst, MA: University of Massachusetts Press, 2002).

Now the woods are filled with rockers,
With heavy hearts and empty coffers.
Hey, man, do you remember last year,
And how I had that great idea?

How we got back to the woods last year.
How we got back to the woods last year.

CRUISKEEN LAWN
from El Ron Maltan
Recorded in Edmundston, New Brunswick[45]

Let the farmer praise his grounds as the huntsman
    does his hounds.
Let them boast all the deeds they have done.
But I more blessed than they pass each happy night and day
On my lovely little Cruiskeen lawn.

Oh, my grandpa and all his sons took up arms to fight
    the Huns
Just to show the devil what side our god was on.
They returned one happy morn to rest their limbs
    all scarred and shorn
On their lovely little Cruiskeen lawn.

When I gave up the drink they referred me to a shrink
Just to discover what father and mother might have
    done wrong.
Though my desires are sublimated I would never
    be alienated[46]
from my lovely little Cruiskeen lawn.

---

45   I recorded El Ron Maltan outside of Dooly's pool hall. After he sang and played
for me, Mr. Maltan recounted how both Charles Dickens and Oscar Wilde once
gave lectures in the former vaudeville theatre across the street, as stops on
their grand North American tours. This marvelous building sadly no longer
stands, according to a recent email message from my informant. May this
blatant disregard for historical memory be a stain on the consciences of the
members of the Edmundston City Council. On which, see Carolyn Hardy, *The
Politics of Forgetting: Class, Regionalism, Gentrification, and Social Movements in
Canada* (Montreal, QC: Black Thorns Press, 2012).

46   "Sublimation" refers to the transferal or translation of frustrated desires into
an idea, object, or activity. Sigmund Freud, *Civilization and its Discontents* (New
York, NY: WW Norton, 2010).

While the boys go drink and roam I would rather stay
     at home
and roundup the wild oats till they are gone.
But if they should reappear then they'll meet my old
     John Deere[47]
On my lovely Cruiskeen lawn.

My wife she loves her flowers she could weed their
     beds for hours;
She works from the moment the dark becomes the dawn.
But when autumn's cold winds blow then her pretty
     flowers go
While still thriving is my Cruiskeen lawn.

If life is just a game then tragedy is just a name,
For the rules you make up as you go along.
All your winnings and your wealth can be measured by
     the health
Of your lovely little Cruiskeen lawn.

And when grim death appears after few but pleasant years
I will welcome him as though he was my son
For I know I shall be blessed, have eternal peace and rest
In my lovely little Cruiskeen lawn.

---

47 John Deere is one of the most respected brands of tractor produced in the
world. The machine indicated in this version of "Cruiskeen Lawn," however,
may rather have been a lawnmower. See Dwight Corfu, "Hitching a Ride: Tractors, Trailers, RVs, and Large Vans in Canadian Folk Songs," *Canadian Folkloristics Bulletin* 39, no. 1 (1999): 333–339.

IS THE LIFE OF A MAN ANY MORE
THAN THE LEAVES?

from Andrew Sisk

Recorded in Montreal, Quebec

I've seen the time pass over me.
And I am a witness to the flowing of the sea.
And I know my children will bury me.
Like my daddy before me, it'll come eventually.

So, I say, children, why do you cry?
Don't waste your time asking why.
No one knows what's on the other side.
Just like all things around you, it's the way it has to be.
I see the cold seasons coming, I hear the funeral bells ring.[48]
What is the life of a man any more than the leaves?

In the town that I call home,
There is a tree that has weathered storms.[49]
Beneath its branches I have grown,
And all around it the people I have known.
And, like the seasons, I've seen them come and go,
Dropped away all the ones I love to know.
What is the life of a man any more than the leaves?

---

48 According to Tina Flusser, the bell, and the ringing of bells, are perhaps the most persistent, rich, and complicated images in the long history of Canadian folk song. Tina Flusser, *Ring my Bell: On the Ringing of Bells in Folk Song in Canada* (Waterloo, ON: Wilfrid Laurier University Press, 2001).

49 Mark that the metaphorical rendering of the storms and the tree, and their relationship to the land and surrounding community, is less an indication of character than a literal description of folkloristic Pentecost. Gale Ledbetter, "Deep Sound, Deep Spirit: Immanence in Balladry in Southwestern Ontario," *Hootenanny* 1001, no. 3 (2001): 1–30.

BIG ROCK CANDY MOUNTAINS

I did not yet know it, but I was on the verge of total break-through, the dialectically synthetic stage of absolute folk, when I arrived at the Banff Centre in the summer of 2011 as an artist-in-residence.[50] My proposed project entailed writing liner notes for a forthcoming anthology album; I thus planned to spend my studio time reading histories of Canadian folk song and sketching analytical impressions inspired by the songs I had gathered to date, with the ultimate aim of producing a text to guide future listeners through my recordings, to situate each song within the surrounding fabrics of history and culture.

The degree to which tasks of quantitative completion can result instead in qualitative metamorphosis, however, was not yet clear to me.[51] Banff would profoundly alter my path.

It was again Dr. Bronnley who had forwarded the call for applications to the residency, the broader theme of which was art and utopianism.[52] "FYI—Hebdige residency in the mountains," he had written. Dr. Bronnley and I were by this point in relatively open hostility, the student no longer meek or mild, silently scribbling the scholarship or DVD recommendations of the mentor for future use; on the contrary, this student was now constantly bristling at the teacher's reactionary

---

50 Because, woefully, there were no folklorist-in-residence programs at the Banff Centre.

51 Friedrich Engels, *Anti-Duhring*, trans. Emile Burns (Moscow: Co-operative Publishing Society of Foreign Workers in the U.S.S.R., 1934).

52 It is perhaps on the question of utopia where the fault lines in my relationship with Bronnley first began to spread. Whereas Dr. Bronnley took a cynical and nihilistic view of social-political transformation in general, but especially with regards to utopianism, I found a pragmatic and radical energy in maps or diagrams of organizational structures that do not yet exist but might yet. I was persuaded, for example, by Ruth Levitas, *The Concept of Utopia* (Toronto, ON: Philip Allan, 1990).

frameworks. "But *why* is it this way and not another?" I was constantly asking. "What of the historicity, and ideological dimension, of the very views you are now proposing? What of the ideological dimensions of the hoops through which I am required to jump in *this* very program?" I more or less demanded multiple times.[53] Although Dr. Bronnley had come to accept that Staunton R. Livingston was going to be one of my dissertation's objects of study, the topic constituting perhaps a single chapter's worth of material, he was unwilling to budge in his opposition to a Livingstonian approach to the entire project; and on this sticky point we had reached but not yet passed our breaking point. By suggesting a residency that featured, as guest faculty, a canonical popular music scholar in the cultural studies tradition, who might point me toward a discursive-semiotic lens as opposed to an authentic-celebratory one, Dr. Bronnelly was making a final effort to influence my intellectual path in terms of methodology, if only by proxy.

Little did Dr. Bronnley know that Dick Hebdige had taken a decisively Livingstonian turn in his own thinking since the late 1980s, or so it would appear to me; or that he had abandoned the study of media and culture entirely in favour of ancient Greek and Latin literature; or that he would directly embolden me via positive feedback at the dining hall one evening, toward the end of the residency, when I shared ideas about my dissertation proposal in the buffet line.[54] The possibility that I might by then not propose any dissertation at all, as conventionally understood, was under consideration, which I believed would be an implicit embodiment of Livingstonion ontology. "That sounds like an interesting project," Dick said, while plating a spoonful of the scalloped potatoes.

---

53 Fredric Jameson, *The Political Unconscious: Narrative as a Socially Symbolic Act* (New York, NY: Routledge, 2013).

54 See, for example, Dick Hebdige, *Hiding in the Light* (New York: Routledge, 1988).

So, in the end I was happy to have submitted an application to the Banff Centre, for it matters less what one intends to do—whether one is an artist or a writer or a manipulative dissertation advisor—than it matters what gets done in the end.[55]

I must be careful, however. Devoting too much space in the present text to my dogfights with Dr. Bronnley, whether face to face or remote, would not amount to an accurate rendering of the complex transformations rippling across my core during this particular leg of my journey. Enmity can function as an engine of creative destruction.[56] Yet, there are also the abundant wonders in the world, so often obfuscated by daily regimens, which artist residencies in the mountains can reveal.

Where to begin? Not counting a brief layover during that-ketamine-fueled hitchhiking journey to Vancouver a decade earlier to pursue work in the film industry, for the first time I was in the province of Alberta, surrounded by snow-capped Rockies and by ferocious, noble beasts. For the first time I was considered an *artist*—with the ID card to prove it—and was being pampered as such, from my roomy studio in the ceramics wing with wall-sized windows, gazing down to the valley below, to meals and bed prepared daily, and the glass-enclosed pool open for night swims among the stars. Furthermore, my fellow travellers were emerging and established artists who ran the gamut of both emerging and established disciplines. Banff was thus very much like utopia proper, as enticingly if fleetingly described by a young Karl Marx in his *Economic and Philosophic Manuscripts of 1844*.[57]

Given the immensity of the resources and their adaptability to folkloristic pursuits, it might seem peculiar that I had not heard much about the Banff Centre before I clicked on

---

55   John Dewey, *Art as Experience* (New York, NY: Capricorn Books, 1934).

56   Karl Marx and Friedrich Engels, *The Communist Manifesto*, trans. Samuel Moore (Halifax, NS: Fernwood, 1998).

57   Karl Marx, *Economic and Philosophic Manuscripts*, translated by Martin Milligan (Moscow: Foreign Languages Publishing House, 1961).

the hyperlink sent by Dr. Bronnley. But honestly, the Centre had not been on my radar. The extensive holdings at their library and archives in both music and Canadian cultural history had escaped my notice. The sacred backdrop and the degree to which artists, writers, and even rock stars had found inspiration there was also unknown to me. Further, no one had described, for example, the urban legends of appetitive artists attending only to have their salacious urges lead to the destruction of preconceived notions, if not entire lives back home. Later, I would learn that one could fill a book with such tales.[58] Thus, communication scholars confident that narratives "about" the world in fact create the very world in question might consider, on the contrary, that I myself was unaware of Banff's legendary stories even while performing a significant role in one exemplary, archetypal variation. Does not, I dare ask, this datum challenge the foundations of their entire theory?[59]

58 Allison Richardson, ed., *Our Tangled Brushes, Our Tangled Limbs: Oral Histories of Excess at the Banff Centre* (Manitoba, MB: University of Manitoba Press, 1991).

59 See, for instance, Ferdinand de Saussure, *Course in General Linguistics*, trans. Wade Baskin (New York, NY: Columbia University Press, 2011).

CORINNA

I had read about Corinna's artwork—piles of obsolesced gar-
bage reanimated through comic spoken-word texts, ambient
music, and pirate radio transmissions—exploring, according
to her interpreters, the mundane delights of life within the
technological detritus of late modernity.[60] I would later learn
that she had read about *The CFL Sessions*, too, and that we had
over sixty Facebook friends in common. We did not formally
meet until the early-morning orientation session on the first
day of our program in Banff, she with her leather jacket and
reusable coffee mug, saucer-sized eyes, and squeaky voice. We
chatted for only a couple minutes about the altitude sickness at
the coffee break. But as our group trudged jovially up the stairs
to the dining hall, I knew I wanted to sit next to Corinna at that
lunch, and at every lunch thereafter, until I died.

Yet, because it was quickly disclosed that Corinna was
joined in monogamous union—parts of a common-area telephone conversation with her partner overheard while Elske,
Demi, and I shared late-night coffee in the ceramics lounge—
our relationship began without ulterior motive, from my
point of view. Popping by her studio on my way to the can-
teen, I would ask whether she needed a coffee, or would
inquire regarding the pleasantness of her day's unfolding if
we ran into one another in the hall. Because both of us were
involved in music—she also played bass in indie rock bands,
back in Winnipeg—we moreover began to share time in one
of the piano huts on the edge of the campus, starting around
the beginning of week two, and decided to join forces on the
construction of a few utopian-themed songs to perform at

---

60 Reviews and features in, for example, *Globe and Mail, Canadian Art, C Magazine,* and *Maclean's.*

our residency's group show.[61] All of this was nothing out of the ordinary, considering the collaboration– and professional network–fostering goals enshrined in the public-facing mission copy of the Banff Centre.[62]

Additional proof that the platonic limits of the relationship had been accepted is that, on the night that Corinna and I first had sex, in my studio, I had already spent dozens of minutes kissing someone else from the writing program, also in my studio. My roommate Julián had thrown an ironic Victoria Day dance party the same night, making screen-printed posters of the Queen, an arrow-shaped mask superimposed over her eyes. Combined with word-of-mouth buzz, Julián's advertisement drew dozens of guests to the celebration: modern dancers, musicians, actors, and staff. We busted moves to LCD Soundsystem and various soul hits while Julián, in time with the groove, manically scrubbed with a plume of steel wool through the endless layers of white paint on his studio walls, so that he might "transport" the rowdy gathering, as he put it, "back through the archive, back through time." The harder Julián scrubbed, down through decades of artist-in-residence sediment, the louder we cheered.

All of which is mere setup, it turns out, to me encountering Corinna back in the residence foyer in the wee hours of the morning, mentioning that I had lost my glasses. "Did you

---

61 At this point, my musical skills were yet in their infancy period. Yet, one of the visual art department technicians lent me her ukulele, among the most forgiving and accessible of folk instruments. See Matthew D. Thibeault and Julianne Evoy, "Building Your Own Musical Community: How YouTube, Miley Cyrus, and the Ukulele Can Create a New Kind of Ensemble," *General Music Today* 24, no. 3 (2011): 44–52. Another instance of prognostication: this self-sacrificing technician hailed from Dawson City, Yukon.

62 "Banff Centre is a catalyst for knowledge and creativity through the power of our unique environment and facilities in the Canadian Rocky Mountains, our rich learning opportunities, *cross-disciplinary and cross-sectoral interactions*, outreach activities, and performances for the public" [emphasis mine]. The Banff Centre, "The Creative Voice: Strategic Plan 2016–2021" (Banff, AB: Banff Centre, 2016).

check your studio?" she asked, surprisingly concerned. She took my hand and we walked together through the night and through the darkly lit halls of the ceramics floor, and, after rehearsing a cappella by the window the cover song we had been working on, devoured each other on my long, narrow workbench.[63] Corinna would later laugh upon learning that I had "lost" the glasses earlier that night while entering an embrace with the writer—the glasses were on my studio shelf in the end, which we noticed while cleaning up—because Corinna had a sympathetic sense of humour and was consistently able to think past her own petite-bourgeois positionality, the latter of which is simply irresistible.

The reader of the present text can likely see where this is going, which is that Corinna had much to do with my looming epiphanies, described in greater detail below. Although conclusions often seem easy or self-evident once written down or sent to the printer, however, these revelations came only through difficult intellectual and emotional labour. More specifically, the closer I moved to Corinna, the farther away she sounded, as though we were playing tug-of-war *and* Whac-A-Mole simultaneously.[64] We shared times of vulnerability and tenderness, such as the ponderously passionate morning during our overnight trip to Calgary, where Corinna had business with an art dealer. Sucking and licking on the bed, squeezing and penetrating in the shower, holding and caressing on the bed once more, both now freshened and robed, and therefore again with the fucking. Not only was I growing attached, but this was the first time that I had felt attachment as such, having never slept with the same person more than

---

63   Talking Heads, "This Must Be the Place (Naive Melody)," track #9 on *Speaking in Tongues*, Sire, 1983, LP.

64   Marshall McLuhan incidentally referred to the boomerang effect of such media interactions as "the reversal of the overheated medium." Marshall McLuhan, *Understanding Media: The Extensions of Man* (Corte Madera, CA: Ginko Press, 2003), 51–60.

once. But Corinna, at least until our teary farewell on that early summer morning of the residency's end, responded to any emotional advances with various sorts of stiff-armed tactics, which would lead to me ignoring her completely, which would lead to her advancing once again. And perhaps it was not so easy to tell who had started any given iteration of the cycle. Is there a word or phrase that better connects love, art, war, folklore, and football than avant-garde?

This roller coaster ride could even be played and replayed again over the span of a single night. One time, for example, my independence was conveyed at a wine and cheese event—I believe this was following Dick's public lecture—by heavy flirtation with the beautiful Dutch sculptor, Lotte.[65] Yet, only two hours later, in the Centre's corporatized airport-style lounge, I found myself interrupting Corinna's close conversation with a handsome jazz instructor from the States, imploring her, when the jazzman left for a cigarette, to come by my room at 3:15 a.m. Goaded on by a gathering of fellow performance artists in the corner, Julián had just drunkenly agreed to dress himself in all of the articles of clothing that he had packed for Banff simultaneously, and thus attired to hike Sulphur Mountain—the highest of surrounding summits—with a group of hearty alpinists. They were departing at three to watch the sun rise.[66] A rare opportunity, I explained,

---

65 Dick's lecture consisted of a brilliant analysis of swimming pools in American culture—sites both of cleanliness and comfort, he argued, but also of death and putrefaction. For a published version of at least a portion of Dick's presentation, I believe, see Daniell Cornell, ed., *Backyard Oasis: The Swimming Pool in Southern California Photography, 1945-1982* (Munich: PRESTEL, 2012).

66 Julián's art practice throughout his residency at the Banff Centre involved durational performance, with or without audio-visual documentation. One day, for example, he made a video recording of himself checking email for eight hours straight. Yet, he often took his practice beyond the studio walls, regularly attempting, for example, to eat full portions of all the desserts at the buffet table, which took a full dinner plate to transport, and insisting that this was a performance, on which point I tend to agree. Peggy Phelan, "The Ontology of Performance," in *Performance*, ed. Philip Auslander (New York, NY: Routledge, 2003), 320–335.

for us to have a bedroom to ourselves. "Okay," Corinna said, I can now hear, with exasperation.

I was soon lying under my sheets in covert anticipation while Julián slowly, clumsily stretched shirt after shirt, sock after sock, and pant leg after pant leg onto his stiffening, expanding figure. But Corinna never arrived. "That was fucking pointless," Julián gasped, exhausted, when he returned around seven, me still in bed, softly crying. Later that morning, however, Corinna entered my studio without knocking, and took me into her mouth, and between her bountiful breasts, without saying a word, and we were both forgiven.

SATURDAY MORNING CARTOONS
from Klaas Dyck
Recorded in Leamington, Ontario[67]

Every day I rise at a quarter to seven;
'Bout an hour or two after you.
The crops are in and the crops are a-growing,
And there's very so much work to do.

You're down in the barn and I'm over in the orchard.
Then you're out in the field and I'm headed to town
For business at the bank and a beer in the tavern.
'Cause we're heavy with debts and I'm ready to drown.

But this is how it goes when the rain is a-blowing.
This is what we do when a storm comes through.
We lay by the fire, our faces a-glowing,
Like Saturday morning cartoons.[68]

After noon we'll head out later;
But only if the sun comes through.
The pepper patch could use some hoeing.
Tonight, maybe a BBQ.

But this is how it goes when the rain is a-blowing.
This is what we do when a storm comes through.
We lay by the fire, our faces a-glowing,
Like Saturday morning cartoons.

---

67 I stumbled upon this ever-fresh tune sung to the melody of "Johnson's Hotel" on the outskirts of Leamington, the foamy shores of Erie in the distance. Leamington remains a complex site of hybrid folklore generation. I recommend that all aspiring folk song collectors among my readership add the town to their list.

68 Yet another folk song that Dale Ricks would no doubt simply pass by on account of his misconceived understanding of authenticity. See, for instance, Dale Ricks, "Tradition Matters: A Plea for Discernment in the Field," *Journal of Canadian Folklore* 634, no. 3 (2007): 99–101.

STONES IN MY PASSWAY
(Or, Notes Toward a Dissertation Proposal)

A professor—or stockbroker or CEO—sits at their desk behind a networked personal computer. Pointing and clicking, typing and sipping from a takeout coffee cup, they input symbols that are instantly converted to electrical impulses and transmitted, through wires and lines, protocols and packet switches, across a global web of informational exchange. And yet, the user sees only the screen, a window—or goalposts—through which inner thoughts or impulses can be directly dropkicked, end over end. Whether trading commodities or viewing pornography, the material substance of the networked personal computer thus seems to disappear over the course of the sending and receiving, leaving only the stockbroker, CEO, or professor—and their mind.

Authentic folk song is a spear crashing through the centre of this solipsistic, bourgeois diagram, which is an ideological model that has been promoted for roughly three hundred years, from the birth of Romanticism to Apple advertisements.[69] Not only has it been revealed that the human subject is not technically a discrete individual,[70] but the line between active author and passive medium does not even exist from the point of view of the Livingstonian folk song collector. The user is merely one component among a broader assemblage of creativity cross-wiring humans and

---

69 Thomas Streeter, *The Net Effect: Romanticism, Capitalism, and the Internet* (New York, NY: New York University Press, 2011). On the ideological dimensions of the interface, see also Jodi Dean, *Democracy and Other Neoliberal Fantasies: Communicative Capitalism and Left Politics* (Durham: Duke University Press, 2009); Alex Galloway, *The Interface Effect* (Malden, MA: Polity, 2012); Katherine Hayles, *How We Became Posthuman: Virtual Bodies in Cybernetics, Literature, and Informatics* (Chicago, IL: University of Chicago Press, 1999).

70 Félix Guattari, *The Machinic Unconscious: Essays in Schizoanalysis*, trans. Taylor Adkins (Los Angeles, CA: Semiotext(e), 2011).

non-humans, plants and animals, digits and indexes, beings and becomings, soils and skies.[71] In the words of Friedrich Nietzsche, not coincidentally inscribed around the same time Charles Babbage and Ada Lovelace swiftly opened the floodgates of computation with their invention, the Analytical Engine: "Our writing tools are also working on our thoughts."[72]

Thinking of communication in this way is a Canadian tradition, too, of which the economist Harold Adams Innis is often cited as progenitor. He made his name in the 1930s through the production of complex analyses of the fur and cod industries, in which he argued that colonialist desires had imprinted themselves on the geopolitical formation of Canada.[73] But in the final stages of his career, and much to the consternation of his colleagues at the University of Toronto, Innis courageously broke beyond his home discipline's entrenched boundaries. He sought to examine the roles of specific media within the coming-to-be and falling apart of the great world-historical civilizations, from Sumer and Egypt to Greece and Britain, often consulting secondary rather than primary sources out of necessity. Out of necessity because he

---

71 See also Benjamin Bratton, *The Stack: On Software and Sovereignty* (Cambridge, MA: MIT University Press, 2016); Donna Haraway, *Simians, Cyborgs, and Women: The Reinvention of Nature* (London: Free Association Books, 1996); Donna Haraway, *Staying with the Trouble: Making Kin in the Chthulucene* (Durham, NC: Duke University Press, 2016); Shannon Mattern, *Code and Clay, Data and Dirt: Five Thousand Years of Urban Media* (Minneapolis, MN: University of Minnesota Press, 2017); and Alexander G. Weheliye, *Phonographies: Grooves in Sonic Afro-Modernity* (Durham, NC: Duke University Press, 2005).

72 Friedrich Nietzsche quoted in Friedrich Kittler, *Gramophone Film Typewriter*, translated by Geoffrey Winthrop-Young and Michael Wutz (Stanford, CA: Stanford University Press, 1999), 200.

73 Harold Adams Innis, *The Fur Trade in Canada: An Introduction to Canadian Economic History* (New Haven, CT: Yale University Press, 1930); Harold Adams Innis, *The Cod Fisheries: A History of an International Economy* (Toronto: University of Toronto Press, 1954).

was dying.[74] What happens, Innis asked, when new channels or codes arise, such as alphabetic writing or moveable-type printing? How do new media rework past ways of transmitting or sharing information, and thus also past ways of doing and being? The answers, Innis discovered, had to do with nothing more and nothing less than the fundamental yet mutable conceptions of space and time.[75]

Innis got the ball rolling before he tragically succumbed to prostate cancer in 1952. What happened next? Who would keep the ball of Canadian communication theory moving? On one hand, there was indeed the celebrity and CBC darling Marshall McLuhan, also a professor at the University of Toronto, who, it must be admitted, made Innis's insights more easily digestible for mass audiences. In particular, McLuhan benched the method of materialist dialectics in favour of the formalist close-reading techniques that had been soldered to him as a graduate student at Cambridge: "Any hot medium allows of less participation than a cool one, as a lecture makes for less participation than a seminar, and a book for less than dialogue," he wrote, for example.[76] A master of the soundbite in a golden age of soundbites, McLuhan's pop-rhetorical style resonated with the countercultural teenyboppers of the 1960s, none of whom, sadly, had likely read a single sentence of *The Fur Trade in Canada*.[77] "The medium is not more important than the message. The medium is the message!" McLuhan is believed to have exclaimed while being harassed by his idiotic

---

74 For a detailed and engaging biographical account of this period, see Alexander John Watson, *Marginal Man: The Dark Vision of Harold Innis* (Toronto, ON: University of Toronto Press, 2006).

75 Harold Adams Innis, *Empire and Communications* (Toronto, ON: Dundurn Press, 2007); Harold Adams Innis, *The Bias of Communication* (Toronto, ON: The University of Toronto Press, 1991).

76 Marshall McLuhan, *Understanding Media: The Extensions of Man* (Corte Madera, CA: Ginko Press, 2003), p. 23.

77 On McLuhan's reception, see Glen Wilmott, *McLuhan, or Modernism in Reverse* (Toronto: University of Toronto Press, 1996).

students after class, if the sensationalist CBC short film is to be believed.[78]

On the other hand, there was Staunton R. Livingston. It is insignificant whether Livingston influenced Marshall McLuhan or vice versa over the course of their brief student-teacher relationship; it is also insignificant whether or not Livingston had read Harold Adams Innis. The point is that from the traces remaining of Livingston's speeches and lectures, and from his masterpiece in the CFL Sessions, one can extract a Canadian communication theory that slingshots out into uncharted territories, offering new maps and models of the late-modern communicative condition. Like a spiritualist seance facilitator or alchemical spinner of gold, Livingston produced recordings of folk songs with his magnetic tape machine at the same time that he erased himself, not as a creative being, but rather as an individual proprietor of creativity, from the equation.[79]

Why has the work of this visionary folk song collector been so obscured across Canadian arts and letters, not to mention the nepotistic institutions that constitute Canadian folklore? Where is Livingston's *Heritage Minute* episode? Where is Livingston's dedicated broadcast of Radio One's *Ideas*?

To conclude, in this dissertation it will be demonstrated that, by suturing communistic folk song collection with Canadian media theory, Staunton R. Livingston kicked off an

---

78 Historica Canada, *Heritage Minutes: Marshall McLuhan.*

79 "If you were to take the recordings that Livingston made of CFL players in the 1970s, and if you were to lay these magnetic tape recordings across the ground, and if it were possible to see, on tape, the grain of the music, then you would see nothing but this grain on Livingston's tapes. It would not be possible to see, there, the lack that is the opposite of the grains of folk song. This means that to listen to the recordings of Staunton R. Livingston is not to hear a singer who is simply passing on a song. When we observe the path that Livingston has laid out for us, we can hear the singer become something other than a mere channel of a message; we can hear the singer reach toward communion, an instrument for itself but longing for others." Henry Adam Svec, "Dissertation Proposal Defense" (University of Western Ontario, September 12, 2011).

explosive and radical framework that requires faithful reception and delivery. Because, in Livingston's tapes and across the quotations of his speeches, we can find the collection of folk songs reformatted as the giving of gifts. Furthermore, it is possible that this axiom can be applied to the collection of anything. One such gift, it will furthermore be seen, is the determinate and transformative power of communication technology into which Livingston invites us to combine and assemble and merge. Ergo, in this dissertation it will be claimed, with Livingston, that the phonographer (to cite merely one possible case study) is no mere note-taker; the opposite is true.[80] We will see that the phonographer is a shaman, witch, wizard, and revolutionary. Any and all counter-arguments will be anticipated, entertained, and obliterated.

---

80   "To write down music, to write about music, even to put a pen into a sound-scape in front of which music is happening, is to defile Music, with a capital M." Staunton R. Livingston quoted in Peter Skellgord, "What I Can Remember," *Globe and Mail*, Dec 26, 1992, A4.

THE BOLD AND UNDAUNTED YOUTH

I refined the plan for my dissertation proposal performance upon my return from Banff and transmitted it to my committee members one warm September afternoon on a bellyful of coffee and pastries. As the careful and sequential reader of the present text will have noticed, I had a clear set of strong hypotheses and, although a clear methodology was not identified, the research itself obviously required investigation of methodological procedures as such: Why have the contributions of Staunton R. Livingston been excluded from the discursive traditions of the field of folklore? What does Staunton R. Livingston have to offer the field of communication studies—and humanity? According to the criteria propounded by virtually every guidebook for writers of dissertations I have consulted—including those lent to me by Dr. Bronnley—this was promising work and should have been given, alongside general constructive criticism, a green light.[81]

Let it also be known that the dissertation proposal was not exactly a famous hurdle in the general trajectory of the average PhD student in the Department of Communication Studies at the University of Western Ontario. Aside from plagiarism or general delinquency, it is true that a couple of trials in the program had proven it possible to flunk out, the comprehensive examinations being the most common. At least, a horror story or two circulated over pints at the Grad Club of petty professors having gone sour on their formerly promising proteges, dropping the blade in the form of a ritualized and *ressentiment*-soaked onslaught in

---

81   See, for example, Kate L. Turabian, *A Manual for Writers of Research Papers, Theses, and Dissertations*, 7th Edition (Chicago, IL: University of Chicago Press, 2007).

the examination room.[82] But I was not writing my comps or even defending my dissertation; this was a minor check-box, merely a formal opportunity to solicit feedback from the professoriate before proceeding with the project. There were no horror stories yet in circulation about botched dissertation proposal defenses.

I must additionally flag that, up until this point, my general performance in graduate school was no less than consistently stellar. I had already published two peer-reviewed academic articles, with a third forthcoming, and passed my written comprehensive exam with flying colours, with one professor even whispering to me in a stairwell that she had "heard through the grapevine" about my submission's publishability, which was uncommon.[83] And the orals a few months later were a true cakewalk, on account of my maturing abilities as a tactician amid the fog of war.[84] Two of my committee members fell into bitter debate *with each other* during the exam, thereby exhausting most of the allotted time. I recall reaching for a Danish—Bronnley tended to bring Danishes for such events, I will give him that—then sitting back to watch the sparks, the battle having something to do with the French reception of Heidegger. "You have no conception of death,"

---

82 These gothic tales functioned by bonding their audience together in fellowship, but also by further sanctifying the legitimacy of the rituals themselves. According to communication theorist Ernest Bormann, this phenomenon of group cohesion through shared narratives and images is known as "symbolic convergence." See Ernest Bormann, "Symbolic Convergence Theory," in *Small Group Communication Theory & Practice: An Anthology*, 8th Edition, eds. Randy Hirokawa, Robert Cathcart, Larry Samovar, and Linda Henman (Oxford: Oxford University Press, 2003), 39–47.

83 Henry Adam Svec, "Becoming Machinic Virtuosos: *Guitar Hero*, *Rez*, and Multitudinous Aesthetics," *Loading...* 2, no. 2 (2008); Henry Adam Svec, "'The Purpose of These Acting Exercises': The Actors' Studio and the Labours of Celebrity," *Celebrity Studies* 1, no. 3 (2010): 303–318; Henry Adam Svec, "'Who Don't Care if the Money's No Good?': Authenticity and The Band," *Popular Music and Society* 35, no. 3 (2012): 427–445.

84 See Carl von Clausewitz, *Vom Kriege* (Berlin: Dümmlers Verlag, 1832).

the external examiner from Philosophy shot at Dr. Bronnley while packing up his laptop.

Therefore, I was confident the problem with my proposal had nothing to do with my ideas. The problem had to do with an incompatibility and a tragic lack of critical reflexivity on the part of the university as an institution. For the choices made in presenting my proposal, germanely grounded in the conceptual contours of the subject matter, were simply not comprehensible from the lofty vantages of the so-called ivory tower. I was like a fiddle or jaw harp, a drum or harmonica, emitting a rich and textured frequency; meanwhile, on the other side of the room, the university was trying to transcribe my rich sounds onto tinfoil.[85]

It does not matter what exactly was said or sung in that boardroom as I planted myself, solidly, in front of Dr. Bronnley and his straw colleagues. They wore tweed jackets and ties and power suits, while I defiantly donned my grandfather's faded striped-green golf shirt, as though draped by the red flag of permanent revolution. I will note that the stuffy contempt on Bronnley's doughy white face, of which I was unafraid, was ultimately backed by a reserve army of institutional power. But more detailed description of the fallout from my already mythologized stand can be left to local historians.[86] What remains significant is that on that day—in that moment—I was no longer even myself. I was done with collecting the songs of the folk, and carrying the information around on my portable recording device, as though carrying a canoe, *à la portage*. It was now time for the folk to carry me.

---

85 Tinfoil was the original sound-recording inscription surface used in Edison's prototype for the phonograph. See Oliver Read and Walter Leslie Welch, *From Tin Foil to Stereo: Evolution of the Phonograph* (Carmel, IN: HW Sams, 1959).

86 Who might begin, as they frame their methodology, with the notion of "thick description." Clifford Geertz, "Deep Play: Notes on the Balinese Cockfight," *Daedalus* 101, no. 1 (1972): 1–37.

THE HOBO'S GRAVE
from Ron Leary[87]
Recorded in Windsor, Ontario

Along the side of the road I've been walking
From job to job,
Looking for anything that'll keep me surviving.
Been too long that I been broken.

There's an unmarked grave that is cov'ring
Me after all these years.
I could never amount to nothing,
No effort could move me forward.

But I'll lie free,[88]
I'll lie free,[89]
I'll lie free,[90]
I'll lie free.[91]

---

87 Although originally from Woodstock, Ontario, Ron Leary has spent much of his life in Windsor, which is where I extracted this song. I would like to point out here that Mr. Leary has been a great help in my journeys, often messaging me to let me know about new possible informants and singers. He has even been so kind as to let me open for him as a lecturer, which, however, I will be the first to admit, was not in his best interest.

88 See Søren Kierkegaard, *The Concept of Anxiety*, trans. Reidar Thomte (Princeton, NJ: Princeton University Press, 1980).

89 See Georg Lukács, *History and Class Consciousness: Studies in Marxist Dialectics*, trans. Rodney Livingstone (Cambridge, MA: The MIT Press, 1971).

90 See Jean-Paul Sartre, *Critique of Dialectical Reason, Volume 1*, trans. Alan Sheridan-Smith (New York, NY: Verso, 2004).

91 See Herbert Marcuse, *An Essay on Liberation* (Boston, MA: Beacon Press, 1969).

part three

SONGS OF
THE CLOUD

STRANGE THINGS DONE

Dozens, if not hundreds, of songs and stories have been written referencing the midnight sun, that poetic moniker for the durability of daytime in the north in the spring and summer months, produced by the shape and position of Earth in relation to the sun. For residents of the Arctic Circle, the rhythm of the region's solar calendar is stamped into the sensorium as early as childhood, one imagines, thus forming a general gestalt, or landscape of life; in the winter there is darkness, and in the summer, light. But for intrepid voyagers like Jack London or Robert Service, the transgression of late afternoon into night, though initially invigorating, leads to all manner of psychic and somatic disturbances.[1] Which have been transformed time and again into lasting literary art.[2]

Precise explanation of the phenomenon is beyond my area of expertise. My best hypothesis is that the midnight sun discombobulates because it erases a fundamental certainty of society as it exists in London, Paris, or Dresden. As the anthropologist Claude Lévi-Strauss once observed, the human brain operates by mapping binary distinctions onto the diverse, variegated tissues of reality.[3] And what binary distinction is starker than that between day and night? To lose this anchoring landmark is to feel truly adrift, like ice-skating in a

---

1   See Karin Sparring Björkstén, Peter Bjerregaard, and Daniel F. Kripke, "Suicides in the Midnight Sun—A Study of Seasonality in Suicides in West Greenland," *Psychiatry Research* 133, no. 2-3 (2005): 205–213.

2   See, for instance, Robert Service, *Songs of a Sourdough* (Toronto: William Briggs, 1909). However, "literary" should be understood in the broadest sense, including the labours also of economists, sculptors, programmers, and even cover band musicians.

3   "[T]he purpose of myth is to provide a logical model capable of overcoming contradictions (an impossible achievement if, as it happens, the contradiction is real)." Claude Lévi-Strauss, "The Structural Study of Myth," *The Journal of American Folklore* 68, no. 270 (1955): 443.

cyclone. Yet, the relative immovability and distinctive functioning of chirographic linguistic systems have performed as salvation, or cure.[4]

When I spent several weeks in Dawson City as part of a self-directed personal retreat in the late spring and early summer of 2013, the wide range of emotions and energies generated by the midnight sun overcame me at various points and in varying combinations. The first week spent in Whitehorse, for example, where I waited patiently for my driver to finish some undisclosed business before transporting me on the six-hour ride to Dawson, was literally awesome. Wandering the rustic streets and cavorting in the local taverns, dipping my feet in the coolest and clearest of streams, and then stumbling back to my hotel room by the airport—everything was illuminated, a shadowless bounty of grasses, trees, and sky. It was nearly possible to leap atop the firmament itself.

If one fast-forwards to my final days in the Yukon, roughly a month and a half later, one finds a very different child of the sun. Having spent the preceding weeks building a technological system that would substantially challenge hegemonic modes of folk song collection, I was by then frazzled, completely frayed. To be clear, the manic, solar energy was still flowing, but the oscillations were almost impossible to control. They finally exploded in Dawson vis-à-vis my housemate and ally, Mirek Plíhal, the consequent wounds of which have been, to this time of writing, unfortunately unable to heal.

More research and greater sample sizes are required, but I have a provisional thesis as to why the creative labour in which I engaged in Dawson with Mirek was incapable of quieting my distressed mind. Writing and print, as Livingston well knew, fostered the fixity, categorization, and linearity that define modernity. Computers instead revel in recombination, modularity, and liquidity; therefore, the binary foundations

---

4   Walter Ong, *Orality and Literacy: The Technologizing of the Word* (New York: Methuen, 1982).

of digital machines (ironically) thus do not determine the epistemological confidence determined by books, and even sound recordings, in their prime.[5] In other words, and in spite of the great obstacles within both artificial intelligence and folkloristic theory hurdled by Mirek and myself in Dawson, a cataclysmic and positive feedback loop was additionally engendered among myself, others, and environment, which by design spun quickly out of control.[6]

Staunton R. Livingston's claim to the 1968 gathering of the Canadian Folkloristics Association—"If you want to make an omelette, you are going to need to break some eggs"—offers partial but not complete consolation.[7] Is it not sometimes better to instead allow the chickens to live, and to grow, and to hatch their own eggs?

---

5 On the fixity of print, I draw here on Marshall McLuhan, *The Gutenberg Galaxy* (Toronto: University of Toronto Press, 1962). On the modularity of digital media, I draw on Katherine Hayles, *How We Became Posthuman* (Chicago: University of Chicago Press, 2006); Maurizio Lazzarato, *Signs and Machines: Capitalism and the Production of Subjectivity* (Los Angeles, CA: Semiotext(e), 2014); Pierre Lévy, *Becoming Virtual: Reality in the Digital Age* (New York, NY: Basic Books, 1998); Lev Manovich, *The Language of New Media* (Cambridge, MA: The MIT Press, 2001).

6 John Bonnett, "The Flux of Communication: Innis, Wiener, and the Perils of Positive Feedback," *Canadian Journal of Communication* 42, no. 3 (2017): 431–448.

7 Staunton R. Livingston quoted by Eli Walchuck quoted in Lynne Wood, "Canada in the 1960s," *Local Histories* 3, no. 4 (2000): 12–17.

I WISH I WAS A CAT IN THE TREE[8]
by LIVINGSTON™

All cats are grey in the dark.
All cats are grey in the dark.
All cats are grey in the dark,
And sometimes in the light.

Cats, they're like a flower
Called "Lily of the Valley."
Small and sweet
And there are so many.

And cats, they're like a river
Flowing through the country.
They bend and they fall,
And came from something.

And cats, they're like a movie
In the theatre.
They begin,
And there's an ending.

---

8 An obvious allusion to Bascom Lamar Lunsford's classic, "I Wish I Was a Mole in the Ground," which is included on Harry Smith's highly influential *Anthology of American Folk Music* (New York, NY: Folkways, 1952).

All cats are grey in the dark.
All cats are grey in the dark.
All cats are grey in the dark,
And sometimes in the light.

And cats, they're like a fruit
Called "peaches."
Soft and sweet,
Hangin' in warm breezes.

&8*&###########6969[9]

All cats are grey in the dark.
All cats are grey in the dark.
All cats are grey in the dark,
And sometimes in the light.

---

9 I have refrained from excising, from the small sample of songs presented in this book, LIVINGSTON™'s so-called glitches. I am sure that this will not persuade many of my professional folklorist readers, among whom the technical sheen of LIVINGSTON™ is practically a poison, but it is worth pointing to the school of media artists out there, for whom glitches are not simply errors or noises, but for whom glitches constitute the raw materials of artistic production—like paints or pencils in their own right—which is a properly Livingstonian philosophy of art. Caleb Kelly, *Cracked Media: The Sound of Malfunction* (Cambridge, MA: MIT Press, 2009).

I COULDN'T HEAR NOBODY PRAY

The reader of the present text should know that I was not exactly in tip-top shape when my plane touched down at the Erik Nielsen Whitehorse International Airport. There were pains in my chest whenever I permitted myself to think, for example, about the always-already elusive meaning of my life; my immediate problems were simultaneously scholarly, creative, and personal.

In terms of professional standing, I was able to rebound from my defeat against Bronnley. Departmental policy permitted a second attempt at the dissertation proposal defense in the event of a failing grade; and although there was not a policy explicitly permitting the alternation of advisors after a first attempt, and such a move was highly unusual at this late stage of the progression, neither was there a policy prohibiting the practice.[10] Bronnley and I would thus meet only one more time as advisor–advisee, he not having realized beforehand that this was the end. "First, you are going to need to read "*A Star Is Born* and the Construction of Authenticity" by Richard Dyer, which I hope will give you some idea as to what analysis looks like in this field," he said, flagrantly impatient since our public crisis.[11] Dr. Bronnley suggested several other titles as well, each of which I wrote down for old time's sake, each of which has proven useful.[12] During a natural break in

---

10 University of Western Ontario Communication Studies Department, "PhD Program Graduate Student Handbook, 2008–2009," 2008.

11 Richard Dyer, "*A Star is Born* and the Construction of Authenticity," in *Stardom: Industry of Desire*, ed. Christine Gledhill (New York, NY: Routledge, 2003), 155–163. Dyer examines the subtle cues by which Judy Garland evokes images of sincerity and authenticity across her films and star texts.

12 Erica Brady, *A Spiral Way: How the Phonograph Changed Ethnography* (Jackson, MS: Jackson University Press, 1999); Edward M. Bruner, "Abraham Lincoln as Authentic Reproduction: A Critique of Postmodernism," *American Anthropologist* 96, no. 2 (1994): 397–415; Johannes Fabian, *Time and the Other: How Anthropology Makes its Object* (New York, NY: Columbia University Press, 1983);

his pontification on the inferiority of the Chicago citation style, I stood and shook his hand, the performative closing of both the conversation and our relationship.[13] "Your service is no longer required," I said. And that was that. I no longer needed his input—nor his signature.

I am not sure that my subsequent dissertation advisor, one of the wisest and kindest people I have ever met, would be comfortable with discussion in the present text of their highly influential scholarship or warm personality.[14] I will state that, although their criticism of my approach to Livingston was similar to that which Bronnley had consistently offered, something about their demeanour helped me, gently, to draw conclusions on my own terms. Over coffee during one of our first meetings at the Grad Club, my new advisor simply pointed out that it is difficult to analyze the work of a theorist who did not write anything down. This, after I began to really think about it, seemed unavoidably true.

What, then, could I research? I was in my final year of funding and tuition remission. Even though I had not yet needed to take on any debt as a graduate student, living for free as I was in my subterranean dwelling, I was running out of road—and ideas.

Things were going no better for me in the folklore department. I had released my second anthology, *Folk Songs of Canada Now*, which consisted of the strongest field recordings I believed myself yet to have gathered.[15] I had toured

---

and James Lastra, *Sound Technology and the American Cinema: Perception, Representation, Modernity* (New York, NY: Columbia University Press, 2000).

13 J. L. Austin, *How to Do Things with Words* (Oxford, UK: Oxford University Press, 1975).

14 This despite the fact that I have taken great pains to obscure the identities of the people to which my book refers, in addition to insisting to my publisher that the text be categorized as "fiction" as a precautionary legal measure.

15 The title mischievously alluded to a classic collection by Edith Fulton Fowke. Edith Fulton Fowke, *Folk Songs of Canada* (Waterloo, ON: Waterloo Music Co., 1954). For the online version of my collection, see Henry Adam Svec, *Folk Songs of Canada Now*, http://www.folk songsofcanadanow.com.

the recording, lecturing about and presenting my findings in all sorts of venues across the country, from pubs and coffee shops to libraries; the *Globe and Mail* had even declared the recording their "Disc of the Week."[16] The project also received the standard CBC coverage.[17] However, I was beginning to grow uncomfortable with the entire premise of the project. Had I really managed to collect the folk songs of Canada? My inherited ambitions were starting to seem impossible, even insane. Staunton R. Livingston's techno-fetishistic and communistic praxis had offered an aestheticized way of sidestepping pressing questions of culture, if not class and solidarity; I believed—and believe to this day—that there is a latent political potential within Livingston's anti-institutional and magical approach.[18] But faith in my ability to translate his philosophies into a *complete* folk song anthology was shot, to such a degree that I did not even bring a microphone or recording device with me to the Yukon.

To be clear, I had not lost confidence in the folk, only in myself. It might be most accurate to state that I had lost confidence in the position of folk song collector. I had captured sublime songs, met interesting people, and done my best to cover as much territory as possible. But had I gone far enough? For example, had I not spent too much time in Southwestern Ontario and Atlantic Canada, and not enough time in, say, Calgary? Not to mention Yellowknife? Had I not contaminated the performances of my informants with

---

16 Robert Everett-Green, "Disc of the Week: Rebooting Canada's Folk Songbook, *Globe and Mail*, October 14, 2011.

17 See, for example, Rex Murphy and Henry Adam Svec (guest), "Does Folk Song Matter Today?" *Cross-Country Checkup*, CBC Radio 1, February 2012.

18 "Staunton R. Livingston only accidentally captured the songs of CFL players. What he essentially captured is communication as revolution—the act of moving air for the purpose of plugging into humanity, which is really just another way of saying 'folk song.' Music in the Livingstonian sense is technically beyond data or information as we conventionally understand these terms; it is beyond character or narrative or motivation; it is noise as signal." Henry Adam Svec, "On Livingston's Method," Rhubarb Festival (public lecture, Buddies in Bad Times Theatre, Toronto, 2011).

my irrepressible personal preference for balladry? Were my ears and eyes not too irredeemably contaminated by the patriarchal settler-colonial nation-state of Canada to conduct the complex, sensitive work of folk song collection? Further, could one person—could I—ever go far enough?[19]

The frailties of human life (my own) and the limitations of individual perspective (my own) had never been more apparent to me than in those weeks of early April 2013 that I spent confined to my basement, coming up only for sandwiches at the fascist coffee chain across the street.[20] Mould grew not only on my walls and carpets but also, it very much seemed, on my spirit. Therefore, as the Forest City's speckled snowbanks finally finished bleeding out, I decided I needed a vacation.

To top it all off, dear reader, I had fallen into a dark, heartbreaking kind of love. Corinna and I were continuing to see one another, but she would not tell her partner, nor had she expressed any concrete willingness to seek a separation. Which meant we were having an affair. We met in London or Toronto, or any nearby town to which we could secure a cheap flight, screwing and embracing in hotel rooms, or in my basement, laughing and weeping. It was the most suitable relationship for this freewheeling folk song collector who longed—and longs still—to be free. But sometimes the culturally constructed desire to couple weighed me down, and the melancholy would rise.[21] I was like a wide receiver on a quick hitch pass; at bottom, despite the pleasures and joys of flesh and contact—in general, of communication—I was completely alone.[22]

---

19 See Sandra Harding, *Science and Social Inequality: Feminist and Postcolonial Issues* (Urbana, IL: University of Illinois Press, 2006).

20 See Patricia Cormack, "True Stories of Canada: Tim Hortons and the Branding of National Identity," *Cultural Sociology* 2, no. 3 (2008): 369–384.

21 See Sean Griffin, ed., *Hetero: Queering Representations of Straightness* (Albany, NY: Suny Press, 2009).

22 See, for example, Roland Barthes, *The Pleasure of the Text*, trans. Richard Miller (New York, NY: Hill and Wang, 1975).

For the record, I was dating other people. My missing front teeth had by now been replaced. Coupled with my new weight-lifting regimen, and the appropriately sized clothes that I had begun to purchase, piece by piece, I was, according to Corinna, an attractive and vivacious young man. It was indeed getting easier to meet people. Curators, bartenders, assistant professors, hairdressers, custodians, fellow folklorists... I will refrain from further detail, for my frequent flings around this time had little bearing on the trajectory of my folk song collecting practices. The point here is that I was not heartbroken over Corinna simply because I was starved for human touch.

I had last seen her in mid-February, two months prior to packing my bags for the Yukon. She had flown to Detroit to give a lecture. Her partner was scheduled to join for a few days afterwards, but she had forty-eight hours free at the start for me. Thus, I took the Greyhound south across the rolling, snow-covered fields, and reminisced about our time in Banff, and about how I wanted my life to look—trying to think harder, perhaps, than I had ever thought before. I wiped away my tears with Subway serviettes. But as we crossed over the bridge toward that iconic concentration of surplus-value extraction, a colony of industrial cathedrals, my mind remained blanker than a fresh reel of magnetic tape.[23] I had no idea what I could, should, or would do. And I had no idea what was coming.

---

23 Detroit was thus appropriately a key focus for the expansion of the proletar-
ian folk song movement of the 1930s and 1940s in the United States, beyond
New York City. Serge Denisoff, *Great Day Coming: Folk Music and the American
Left* (Baltimore, MD: Penguin Books, 1973). On broader shifts in the relation-
ship between subjectivity and alienation, see also Michael Hardt and Antonio
Negri, *Empire* (Cambridge, MA: Harvard University Press, 2001).

BURY ME NOT ON THE PRAIRIE[24]
by LIVINGSTON™

I am a lonesome idiot;
Just can't get rid of it.
I been to oceans, I been to ponds,
Been to the prairies and to Yukon,
And I ain't no one;
And I ain't got no one.

One time, in the back of my belly,
There was a longing in me;
It wasn't mine.
I pulled it out and I threw it;
It didn't have nothing to do with
The empty and the echo that I am.

X

   X

You only get one life,
But you gotta live it till you die;
It doesn't matter what you try.
At the end of the road there's a hole
Where they put your body when it's gotten too old,
Sometimes even before,
If you're lucky, then before.

---

24 The title suggested by LIVINGSTON™ for this song was actually "I Am A Weary Immaterial Labourer in a Post-Industrial Informational Wasteland," which I agree is far superior. However, that option elicited an unfortunate amount of laughter from early test audiences back in Ontario, and so a more traditional title was sutured to the text in order to preserve the sanctity of LIVINGSTON™'s soulful composition.

And one time in Alberta
I got to thinking how fertile
Earth can be.
It lasted all of a minute,
Till I came clear through it,
Grounded by a darkness and Calgary.

You only get one life,
But you gotta live it until you die;
It doesn't matter what you try.
At the end of the road there's a hole,
Where they put your body when it's gotten too old,
Sometimes even before,
If you're lucky, long before.

IN THE WILDERNESS

On the ground in Dawson City, it was my old friend Matt Sarty who found a short-term sublet in town, a room in the Macaulay House, a heritage home presently occupied also by a computer programmer named Mirek Plíhal. The latter detail was not discovered until I was dropped by the front steps and wandered inside. "Is it a house? Apartment? Condo???" I had messaged through Facebook in frustration while waiting for my last connecting flight. These were the kinds of questions to which Matt Sarty rarely responded, or to which he responded with cryptic symbols.[25] I am unsure whether or not I would have gone to Dawson for my vacation, however, if I had known I would have a housemate. This is significant.

Predictably, my initial week with Mirek on the corner of Princess and Seventh Streets was no honeymoon phase. In order to establish boundaries, I decided—or perhaps this choice was less logically deduced than subconsciously summoned—to mark a disconnect between my life at the house and my life in the public sphere.[26] For example, my first evening in town, after our earlier curt introduction, I passed Mirek in the kitchen but did not say a word, walking directly past to the mudroom, out to meet Sarty and his cortège for an open mic event in the ballroom by the river. When I ran into Mirek later at that very gathering, he expressed regret

---

25 For example, the thumbs-up icon, or the blue ghoulish scream icon. On the nature of iconicity versus indexicality and signification, see Charles Sanders Pierce, "The Sign: Icon, Index, and Symbol," in *Images: A Reader*, eds. Sunil Manghani, Jon Simons, Arthur Piper, (New York, NY: Sage Publications, 2006), 107–109.

26 Which emerges in the eighteenth century, in part, and this is significant, due to the proliferation of printed materials. Jürgen Habermas, *The Structural Transformation of the Public Sphere: An Inquiry into a Category of Bourgeois Society*, trans. Thomas Burger (Cambridge, MA: The MIT Press, 1991).

that we had not gone together. "I was going to invite you, but you rushed off," he said. I shrugged my shoulders and went back to the bar.

I also made it clear that we would not be sharing any silverware or dishes. Assembling a short stack of plates and cutlery by the edge of the counter, my claimed utensils carefully covered with a dishtowel, I verbally indicated the next morning that these items were to be used by me and me alone.[27] After that, there was a tinge of bitterness on his part during our brief and silent encounters, he making tea or toast, for example, while I prepared one of my steadily improving stews. Aside from the soft sounds of clinking, cutting, wiping, or simmering, the sincere din of the local community radio station was the only noise in the downstairs common area.

In casting my mind back to this period, it is as though I was seeking to resist the fortuitous currents of destiny, propelled as I was by pure chance or my own interpersonal inadequacies. Our talents were exactly opposite but complementary, our attitudes and demeanours overlapping and synergistic; together, we had the equipment to accomplish something beyond anything in either of our oeuvres to date. I only needed to accept.

This happened one slow afternoon; I believe it was a Tuesday. Less than a week in, I had already grown bored, not of Dawson's wild nights, but of the daytime hours, when the gold miners and reality television crews plugged away within their respective métiers on this final frontier. I found it onerous

---

27 My deliberate intention, insofar as I reflected upon it at the time, was to continue with the communication of self-determination. However, it is also worth mentioning that I suffer from obsessive compulsive disorder, which, despite the consequent personal difficulties, has been, I believe, an asset in the field of folk song collection. And the data backs up my informed supposition: Jack F. Samuels, O. Joseph Bienvenu III, Anthony Pinto, Abby J. Fyer, James T. McCracken, Scott L. Rauch, Dennis L. Murphy et al. "Hoarding in Obsessive–Compulsive Disorder: Results from the OCD Collaborative Genetics Study," *Behaviour Research and Therapy* 45, no. 4 (2007): 673–686.

to endure until happy hour. I had taken every lunch so far at the Downtown Hotel, ordering the daily special, which lasted a good sixty minutes, an hour and a half with dessert.[28] One day I spent the afternoon reading at the public library; I spent a couple of mornings sitting in the courthouse, where a local man was defending himself against the charge of attempted murder.[29] A disappointingly dull afternoon was whittled away in the local archives, where I searched through short texts published in and around the area, looking for forgotten folk songs.[30] Had I lost even my passion for stacks and piles of documents?[31] I was intrigued by the menacing woods beyond the town's perimeter, but too afraid to leave the settlement. I therefore bounced in this way from establishment to establishment, across the dirt roads and along the antique boardwalks. When I returned to the house that aforementioned Tuesday around four in the afternoon to find Mirek sitting on the living room couch, holding a Coors Light and watching my favourite game-show, my cold armour was adulterated with one decisive blow. "Is this new?" I asked, eying the screen. I sat down.

Mirek had cued a YouTube recording of a past broadcast of *Jeopardy!*[32] Neither standard contest nor tournament special,

---

28 The special was usually a salty or cheesy soup paired with an appropriately cheesy or saucy sandwich. For instance, cream of cheddar-potato might go with the Monte Cristo, or cream of broccoli with the ranchy grilled chicken.

29 Long after I was back south, I was happy to discover that a jury of peers found the man to be innocent, which I applauded. It was two bully cops that had accused the local man, who had chosen to represent himself, of attempting to murder one of *them*; but the cops' story was clearly full of holes, or so it had seemed to me. See Christopher Scott, "McDiarmid Acquitted of Attempted Murder," *Yukon News*, March 5, 2015.

30 I only found the sheet music for two jazz numbers from the 1920s, one about gold mining and the other a horrific, racist serenade, neither of which could be reasonably called folk song from the Livingstonian perspective.

31 One might say that I swapped my archive fever for the cabin strain, which reacts disastrously with certain personalities, resulting sometimes in homicide. See, for instance, Rudy Wiebe, *The Mad Trapper* (Markham, ON: Red Deer Press, 2003).

32 *Jeopardy!*, "The IBM Challenge," directed by Kevin McCarthy, aired on February 14, 2011, ABC.

the episode featured all-time champions Brad Rutter and Ken Jennings tackling a state-of-the-art, artificially intelligent digital machine, WATSON™. I had heard about but not seen the game, which was oddly interspersed with journalistic segments shot on location at the IBM laboratories and hosted by a walking-and-talking Trebek, who explained how the system was wired and on what basic principles it operated. The show was more commercial than canon, on the whole, but the general conceit was mesmerizing. Not long ago, this had seemed to be a science-fiction scenario. Given the complexity of the task in comparison to checkers or chess, for example, a Jeopardy!-playing computer would need rather to read and understand and formulate responses to an almost infinite range of possible question genres and subject areas, through the medium of natural language.[33] And yet, here we were. By the end of the first round, WATSON™ was tied for first place.

In the Double Jeopardy! round, the machine broke away completely. WATSON™ left his sputtering flesh-and-blood challengers, in spite of their verified talent, to eat his silicon-flavoured dust. Mirek and I watched as question after question was translated by this electronic titan straight into cash money, a glowing and ominous icon on a black screen positioned behind the middle podium, which, Trebek patiently explained, was not WATSON™ himself but merely an avatar.[34] "What is violin?" "Alex, what is leprosy?" "Who is Isaac Newton?" "What is gestate?" Even though WATSON™ fumbled the Final Jeopardy! question by answering "What is Toronto???????" when the answer had been Chicago, in a category entitled U.S. Cities, it was a landslide win.

---

33 See Rob High, "The Era of Cognitive Systems: An Inside Look at IBM Watson and How It Works," *IBM Corporation Redbooks* (2012): 1-16.

34 WATSON™ was the size of a room and thus housed in a nearby facility. And yet, perhaps his presence onstage, even if feasible, would have been too disturbing for the audience to witness. William Duncan, "Anomie and Uncanniness in Digital Machinery," *Avatar* 34, no. 4 (2009): 121–129.

Ken Jennings finished with $4,800, Brad Rutter with $10,400, and WATSON™ with a monumental $35,734.

Mirek laughed derisively as the credits scrolled alongside the theme song. "Big whoop-de-do," he said, and made a fast, descending fart noise with his lips. I was intrigued by this attitude, the perplexing confidence, which I did not read as a threat given the vast differences in our stock-in-trade, and an evident lack, despite his gigantic head, of muscle mass. I decided that I could like the guy.

My new friend hopped up as YouTube cycled to a random Trebek interview; he grabbed another beer, and one for me. "What did she say, that scientist at IBM? 'So much data... The question is... How do you get intelligence, not just noise?'"[35] I nodded. "Hmm," he said, and flopped back onto the couch. Mirek picked up a pad of paper from the coffee table, scrawling a note or diagram. We continued to watch *Jeopardy!*-related videos and sip our Coors Lights. We did not speak much—"wow," "phsaw," et cetera—but one could feel the comfort, a trust, building perceptibly.[36]

We headed to The Pit, a local watering hole, after one more beer to dine on fried appetizers, and moved on to whisky. It turned out that Mirek had come to Dawson from Montreal to work on a web-based National Film Board film involving both live-action and animated components—intended cleverly to engage the user/viewer, incorporating aspects, for example, of their location and search history—a film about ghost sightings and stories in Dawson. One of the town's many ghosts allegedly occupied the bygone house we currently shared, which was where much of the live-action filming had been done. Production had closed and Mirek

---

35 Dr. Katharine Frase in *Jeopardy!*, "The IBM Challenge," directed by Kevin McCarthy, aired on February 15, 2011, ABC.

36 I did not apologize, but regretted my earlier shenanigans and knew that he could feel my remorse. Jack Burgoon and Edith Seguin, "Nonverbal Communication in the Area of Forgiveness," *Journal of Proxemics* 50, no. 2 (1993): 222–245.

was presently, like me, recharging his batteries. "I like the rawness of the place," he said, scanning the ancient, wooden tavern with a vague smile as another crew of cadaverous ruffians entered.

Our glasses were filled and refilled, my inhibitions breaking like the Yukon River in spring. A local trio played classic rock and country; "Wagon Wheel," for instance, at least twice. I told Mirek about my life and struggles—about Dr. Bronnley and my defiant persistence within the doctoral program; about my current writer's block and paralyzing fear of plagiarism; about my wild song-collecting journeys; and, of course, about Staunton R. Livingston. "There is something interesting to me about the idea that you could bring about utopia without anyone noticing," I explained, righteously concerned.[37] Mirek listened with care and generosity. I politely reciprocated as he described his achievements in the field of machine learning and his impressions of North America. "A wild land," he said with approval. We also swapped stories about certain unpleasant colleagues we had encountered in our respective disciplines—whom, in my case at least, I was determined to destroy—eventually sharing general hopes and fears as well as our most recent romantic blunders.

It came to feel as though we were fellow travellers. And then, once a certain virtuality was decisively uttered, potential teammates.[38]

It is a convention in the Yukon, perhaps in Alaska too, that

---

37 This excursus required brief explanation of the important distinction between abstract and concrete utopia, as developed by Ernst Bloch. The former is idealist and empty; the latter is structural and revolutionary; but both are good. See Ruth Levitas, "Educated Hope: Ernst Bloch on Abstract and Concrete Utopia," *Utopian Studies* 1, no. 2 (1990): 13–26.

38 Keep in mind that the virtual does not necessarily need to be uttered in order to become real: "Purely actual objects do not exist. Every actual surrounds itself with a cloud of virtual images. This cloud is composed of a series of more or less extensive coexisting circuits, along which the virtual images are distributed, and around which they run." Gilles Deleuze and Claire Parnet, *Dialogues II* (New York, NY: Columbia University Press, 2007), 148.

taverns and pubs have bells by the bar, the ringing of which elegantly transmits the signal that the ringer shall buy a round of drinks for all humans within earshot. I imagine this folk tradition came out of the gold rush days, when lucky miners wanted either to show off or generously donate to their less fortunate colleagues-slash-competitors; the ringing of the bell simultaneously signified triumph, hope, community.[39] The medium stuck around, although it seemed not often to be used now except by American tourists. But that night, mere moments after the barkeep shouted for last call, and approximately twenty minutes after Mirek and I decided to work together in the construction of an artificially intelligent database of Canadian folk music—"a digital organism capable of accessing the totality of the history of Canadian folk music, but also of generating new yet hyper-authentic Canadian folk song-texts via algorithmic agents and compression formats"— Mirek shook his head back and forth, jowls flapping, making again that farting sound, and leapt up toward the bell.[40]

I had never heard a sound as crystalline, as resounding. The noble, hollow-eyed patrons erupted into boisterous cheer and, after their gifts were hastily distributed, stood and raised their glasses to Mirek. He, in turn, raised his to me, the slanted wooden floorboards creaking jubilantly below. The other haggard men and women were saluting the free booze. But they were also, in a way, applauding the digitization of folk music and the authentication of digitality, hooraying as premonition of our victory. The scene makes me smile, still, whenever I think of it.

---

39 See, perhaps, Ken S. Coates, *Land of the Midnight Sun* (Montreal: McGill-Queen's University Press, 2013).

40 Henry Adam Svec, "Artificially Intelligent Machine Generates Authentic Canadian Folk Music" (Press Release), 2013.

GREEN GRASS GROWING ALL AROUND
by LIVINGSTON™

We've got the same eyes.
How'd that happen?
My blood is Slavic;
Yours is Anglo-Saxon.
I guess all kinds of people know how to look sad.

"Hey. Why's your heart beating so much faster than mine?
Are you sick or something?"

"No, that's just how I am. **THAT I AM.$$
My body was built for hunting.
You don't know what I'm capable of!"

We have the same eyes, though,
How'd that happen?
My blood is Slavic;
Yours is Anglo-Saxon!
All kinds of people know how to look sad.
I guess all kinds of people know how to look sad![41]

---

41 One needs not spend long in the comparative study of global folk song to find that LIVINGSTON™'s hypothesis is on the money. See, for example, Richard Polenberg, *Hear My Sad Story: The True Tales That Inspired "Stagolee," "John Henry," and Other Traditional American Folk Songs* (Ithica, NY: Cornell University Press, 2015); L. I. Quan-Lin, "On Taiwan Dialectical Ballads in the Period of Japanese Occupation," *Journal of Anhui University of Science and Technology* 2 (2009): n.p.; Erin Sanders, "It's Easy to Cry: The Musicality of Emotions in Portuguese, French, British, and American Balladry," *Musical Sounds* 43, no. 4 (2008): 333-380.

JACOB'S LADDER

There is a feeling one might discover in the midst of a burst of creative or intellectual mania. The distinctions between morning and afternoon, full and hungry, awake and asleep, recede; there is only the task at hand. It is a wonderful feeling. All other personal, familial, and geopolitical dilemmas fade until what remains is solely the buzz and hum of war against a particular problem.[42] This is the sensation that most warmly marks my memory of the four weeks during which Mirek and I worked together in our atelier in Dawson, fueled mainly by fried and frozen entrees, beer and booze, and the midnight sun.

I argue that one of the key components of our strategy was to establish a clear division of labour, although I do want to point out, if Mirek is reading, that this also became one of the causes of our dissolution.[43] But that separation of tasks, and our particular distribution of tasks between the scientist and the humanist, appeared at first to befit the immense interdisciplinary challenges of the project.[44] We needed to wrap up our respective problems, firmly, from within our respective sets of expertise.

Our quarterback, Mirek, worked mostly at the kitchen table, onto which he had moved his desktop computer; there,

---

42 The phenomenological experience of that which athletes, musicians, writers, and scientists often refer to as "the zone"—a heightened and even shamanic state of focus and energy—is also achievable by patient folk song collectors. Debby Kripke, "The Uses (and Overuses) of Meditation in the Field," *Journal of Applied Folkloristics* 57, no. 1 (2004): 33-34.

43 For thus, regarding one of our earliest arguments, about the sustainability and ethics of the industrial mode of production, I win. See Harry Braverman, *Labour and Monopoly Capitalism: The Degradation of Work in the Twentieth Century* (New York, NY: Monthly Review Press, 1998).

44 Which, in my estimation, is precisely why LIVINGSTON™'s songs were and are light years beyond the work of their contemporaries. See, for instance, Ross Goodwin, *1 The Road* (Paris: Jean Boîte Éditions, 2018). Pathetic.

he tightened and refined the pattern-recognition algorithms and user interface on which he had been working for months prior to his arrival in the North. He shared few details. I had difficulty following his jargon-laden narrations, and he quickly grew tired of translating his tasks into layman's language. Meanwhile, I was stationed on the couch in the living room—a protective offensive guard—perhaps the offensive coordinator—where initially my job was to help sort the pools of information in LIVINGSTON™'s dynamic, intelligent database, uploaded from a heterogeneity of print and online sources.[45]

As I understood it, the purpose of my work was to help LIVINGSTON™ learn how to listen to authentic folk song: to recognize and value, for instance, coherence and tension, consonance and dissonance, surrealist juxtaposition and subversive energy. Specifically, as LIVINGSTON™ scrolled through the texts I amassed—slowly, but only for the sake of my all-too-human perceptual equipment—I inputted, in binary form, bits of information. At regular intervals, that is, I was to click either YES or NO.[46] Once LIVINGSTON™ began to generate its own original works informed by their classified holdings, my job was to send similar feedback, again in binary form: YES/NO. YES/NO. YES/NO...

One could argue that it was therefore my responsibility to "teach" LIVINGSTON™ the boundaries between folk song and non-folk song, signal and noise.[47] This is not how I prefer to see the relationship. For what I saw in LIVINGSTON™ was not a mere implement or subservient tool through which I

---

45 We uploaded, first, the Canadian folk song canon proper (Fowke, Barbeau, Creighton, Svec, etc.). It is our surprising subsequent choices, however, from which LIVINGSTON™ derives its, so to speak, secret sauce.

46 I do know that this is known in AI research as "supervised learning." Antti Rasmus, Mathias Berglund, Mikko Honkala, Harri Valpola, and Tapani Raiko. "Semi-Supervised Learning with Ladder Networks," *Advances in Neural Information Processing Systems* 28 (2015): 3546–3554.

47 E.g., Jim Nash, "The Need for Authority in Contemporary Folkloristics," *Journal of Canadian Folklore* 120, no. 500 (2015): 259–284.

could exercise my power as arbiter or gatekeeper of Canadian folk song; I had already been down that road. What I came to see in LIVINGSTON™—sitting on our beigey floral couch, holding the hardware on my lap, and downing can of Coors Light after can of Coors Light—was a comrade. A friend. A friend made by and in union with another friend, my best friend, working diligently in the neighbouring room to orchestrate bright-green undulating flows of data. Hence, nearly every step of the way, as LIVINGSTON™'s folk song-generating/collecting habits were written or disciplined into its immaterial body, there was only one signal I ever sent: YES. LIVINGSTON™, I said, YES.[48]

The hypothesis, the aspect about which I had become most excited that first night together at The Pit, was that LIVINGSTON™ might achieve a self-reflexive, autopoetic loop of authenticity analogous to that equiprimordially possessed by the folk, if not always possessed by academic Canadian folklorists.[49] LIVINGSTON™ would thus become both folksinger and folk song collector, both practitioner and theorist, both songwriter and song-reader. Both content and medium.[50]

As we inched closer to the end zone, however, I could not help but wonder: What was the fate of the professional, human folklorist in the post-LIVINGSTON™ world? I could not be sure, but admit now that I took satisfaction from the possibility that the discipline might be eviscerated by the blade of a

---

48 Aside from perhaps eight or nine total exceptions, but keep in mind that these were out of thousands upon thousands of messages sent from me to the machine.

49 For a case in point, see Dale Ricks, "The Folk songs of the Youth: Traditional Music at Upper Canada College," *Song Collecting Quarterly* 37, no. 4 (2006): 1–10.

50 It should be acknowledged that we were not the first team to try to digitize the folkloristic enterprise. Alan Lomax, toward the end of his career and life, sought to make it possible for computer users to code and analyze folk musical performances and to analyze the global data crowdsourced by the platform, a tool he called "The Global Jukebox." See John Szwed, *Alan Lomax: The Man Who Recorded the World* (New York, NY: Viking, 2010).

weapon I had helped forge. And, as I lay down each night after a long day of joyful toil, followed by our habitual trip to The Pit for whisky and hot dogs, or whisky and jalapeno poppers, the sunlight splintering through my insufficient blinds, I had a recurring fever dream. I was at sea; Marius Barbeau, Helen Creighton, and Edith Fowke were crowded together in a rickety dory; Dr. Bronnley was for some reason among them (had he been a folklorist all along?); and I was a general, expertly commanding a tall and erect battleship nearby that was blowing them, with shot after shot of cannon balls, into smithereens. All the while, and this was the most disturbing part, I myself sang Canadian folk songs, entirely unaccompanied.[51]

What could it mean? One insight was that LIVINGSTON™ would not soon reach the point at which it would be able to perform its songs. This is—or was, at the time—impossible for even the most advanced of artificial intelligences.[52] LIVINGSTON™ could only export the visual symbols and icons conventionally found on the QWERTY keyboard.

At first, Mirek did not object to my learning and practicing some of LIVINGSTON™'s songs around the house, which I began to do around week three.[53] My skills as singer and guitar player, largely earned through gradual exposure to my folk informants, were rudimentary but passable. Still, I could not have convincingly performed every one of the numbers in LIVINGSTON™'s expanding oeuvre. So, I started to select— unwittingly, I see it now—only the ones that spoke to me on a

---

51 See Helen Creighton, *Maritime Folk Songs* (Toronto, ON: McGraw-Hill Ryerson, 1972).

52 There have been startling developments in this area. In April 2020, for instance, Open AI unveiled Jukebox, "a model that generates music with singing in the raw audio domain." Prafulla Dhariwal, Heewoo Jun, Christine Payne, Jong Wook Kim, Alec Radford, and Ilya Sutskever, "Jukebox: A Generative Model for Music," *arXiv preprint* arXiv:2005.00341 (2020). The sound recordings are both stunning and uncanny.

53 It was through Matt Sarty that I was able to borrow a Yamaha acoustic guitar from a local musician. Again, coordinating the pickup was onerous due to Matt's texting style, but I was nonetheless grateful.

personal level. For example, I was drawn to LIVINGSTON™'s songs about desolation, and indomitability, and to the post-human way LIVINGSTON™ rendered love as a physical matter of supple wires and connectors.[54] LIVINGSTON™'s rich metaphors and stark diction mirrored my world, but also made it strange, impossible; all that had felt necessary and inevitable was now contingent and changeable.[55] For the music, I was simply suturing LIVINGSTON™'s texts to conventional chord progressions in the field of Canadian folk song, which was so easy that I felt driven by a benevolent outside force. The resulting combination was a potent and thoroughly Livingstonian palimpsest of future and past, artifice and nature—and thus LIVINGSTON™ became the name of our creation. I insisted upon it.

But Mirek drew his line in the sand when, in week four, an invitation to present our work to the public in Dawson City materialized. Here was our Alamo—our Austerlitz.

By then, the whole town had gotten wind of the project, maybe because of our often-lubricated confidence and ubiquitous presence on the bar scene. It was emboldening to be acknowledged—fellow people asking me, at the gas station where I purchased my takeout coffee in the mornings, for example, about the latest progress on our "thingamajig."[56] On one hand, I wanted as clearly as possible to communicate the details of our *collaborative* discovery. On the other, I wanted to witness an unsuspecting audience encountering LIVINGSTON™'s philosophy of art and existence, and for our avant-garde bombardment to be recognized from within

---

54　Cf. Rosi Braidotti, *The Posthuman* (Malden, MA: Polity Press, 2013).

55　This is what some Russian literary theorists have referred to as *defamiliarization*. For a Western Marxist inflection of the concept, see Bertolt Brecht, *Brecht on Theatre* (New York, NY: Hill & Wang, 1977).

56　As I have argued elsewhere, there are etymological connections joining the terms gadget, thingamajig, and hootenanny. See Henry Adam Svec, "iHootenanny: A Folk Archeology of Social Media," *The Fibreculture Journal* 25 (2015): n.p.

a legible horizon of aesthetic experience. In order to achieve these tandem goals, I decided that our contribution required a certain amount of data compression.[57]

In spite of the lowness of the stakes, and in spite of the open generosity and kind interest of the inhabitants of Dawson, Mirek was against the idea of me singing a selection of the songs as part of our upcoming demonstration at the Klondike Ballroom. He was also opposed to me contextualizing, in the form of a lecture, our invention as part of the long history of Canadian communistic folk song collection. "Not the greatest idea," he said, frankly.

Mirek's counterproposal, which he sketched on the back of the calendar in our kitchen, was that we instead install LIVINGSTON™ on a few different computer stations throughout the venue, allowing audience members to float in and out, if they so wished, and to witness LIVINGSTON™'s ever-evolving creativity in action through the computer monitor.[58] Eventually our lead programmer would need to deliver a short talk on the broader scientific applicability of supervised machine learning, Mirek said, circling the stage in blue pen. This, however, would not do justice, I argued—and then pleaded—to the rich traditions out of which our LIVINGSTON™ had taken flight.

In general, I want all creatures and things to exist in their own way. But when I perceive a body—whether object or subject—to be intentionally intervening in my path, seeking

---

[57] A quick Google Scholar query reveals that my hypothesis has been taken seriously, not only in folklore, where the validity is obvious, but also in information processing. Te Sun Han, "Folklore in Source Coding: Information-Spectrum Approach," *IEEE Transactions on Information Theory* 51, no. 2 (2005): 747–753. I guess Mirek is not a subscriber of *IEEE Transactions on Information Theory*.

[58] Our conflict therefore had to do with the question of the locus of the work of the artificially intelligent folk song database. The songs themselves, which in the end needed to be heard by humans, were my focus; Mirek's focus was the horsepower of LIVINGSTON™'s archive, or "database aesthetics." Victoria Vesna, *Database Aesthetics: Art in the Age of Information Overflow* (Minneapolis, MN: University of Minnesota Press, 2007).

to dominate my will to their program, my ample reserves of decorum and deference can run low. What I mean is that, once the crack in my bond with Mirek appeared, I was undertrained and underconditioned to attempt any repairs. Roused by the perpetual sun and by our drinking, our debate about how to properly present a hyper-authentic digital folk song database consequently devolved into personal and professional insults, hostile and threatening tirades, and physical pushing beside the top of the stairs in our home. After which, on the thirtieth day, we resolved never to speak to one another again. "Fine" was the last word each of us was to say to and receive from the other.

We still went ahead with the public unveiling of LIVINGSTON™ at the end of my fifth and final week in town, having spent the leadup in our bedrooms alone, passing in silence in the hall, and holding court at opposite ends of The Pit. However, because we resolved to deliver our respective visions simultaneously at the Klondike Ballroom—an arrangement negotiated over emails sent from within the same house—LIVINGSTON™'s northern reception was largely characterized by the pure befuddlement of all in attendance. In fact, Matt Sarty would later inform me that word on the street was that Mirek Plíhal and Henry Adam Svec had co-presented one of the worst concerts and one of the worst product launches the town had ever seen or heard—an update concluded with a laughing-crying emoji.

Contra Matt Sarty, I must be clear that the highs and lows recounted above are, at present, no laughing matter. Would you chortle if the last impression of the sole authentic collaboration you had ever experienced was your buddy staring out the living-room window, his moon-face red, his eyes black and cold, while you waited in the front yard for the six-hour shuttle back to Erik Nielsen Whitehorse International Airport?

The memories I choose to preserve of my endless days with Mirek are of the before-times, when our actualization of

LIVINGSTON™ was not yet a foregone conclusion. The windows open, the early summer breeze wafting through our rustic workshop, the sounds of typing and muttering drifting out from the kitchen, slow fingerpicking or strumming coming from me, the TV on mute. And then, around four in the afternoon, Mirek's chair scratching the floor as and he rose, the fridge opening and closing, and the cracking of a fresh beer as my partner slumped down beside me, exhausted, eager to listen to the songs we had just that day shepherded into the world, as though for the first time, but also as though time were merely a bourgeois illusion.

Of course, LIVINGSTON™ is its own entity too; one day, perhaps the machine will stand in a museum of musical or cultural AI heroes—a museum built by the artificially intelligent conquerors of some upcoming, anti-human genocidal war.[59] As I see it, LIVINGSTON™ is just the name that Mirek Plíhal and I gave to the relationship we forged together, and from which we derived the most strange yet marvelous masterpiece either of us could have fathomed. LIVINGSTON™ is just another name for the overflowing well that is authentic folk song.

---

59 As has been rendered in various science-fictional Hollywood apocalyptic films. See, for example, Dir. James Cameron, *The Terminator* (1984: Hemdale & Pacific Western Productions/Orion).

INSTRUCTIONS TO YOUR
INTEGRATED CIRCUITS
by LIVINGSTON™

At the bottom of a cold valley,
I see you coming through.
The bears are crying and the wolves are praying.
They're moved by love so true.

But somebody somewhere with a great lovemaking manual
Knows what I want to do.
Knows it and has seen it in pictures:
My route to you.

By the edge of a tributary,[60]
I see you howling at the moon.
The water flows but you sit easy,
Humming and singing your tunes.

But somebody somewhere with a great lovemaking manual
Knows what I want to do,
Knows it and has seen it in pictures:
My route to you.

At the end of a dark alleyway,
Can't tell what you'll do,
Whether you're coming to me or leaving;
There isn't any light on you.

But somebody somewhere with a great lovemaking manual
Knows what I want to do.
Knows it and has seen it in pictures:
My route to you.

---

60 Note that there is a double meaning of "tributary" which resonates very much
with Livingstonian Canadian communication theory: (1) a river or stream or
channel; (2) a person who pays tribute (*Oxford English Dictionary*).

TAKING OFF MY GLASSES TONIGHT
by LIVINGSTON™

Through the frosted windows down these tired
   swollen streets
TVs glow and I drive along.
I ain't drank too much yet, just enough to get me out.
I won't be driving home.

I'm taking off my glasses tonight.[61]
I won't need to see tonight.

All dolled up, and this is where they go.
Just of age, or older, I don't know.
And I don't care too much,
I just want to settle down
For the night or until I head home.

I'm taking off my glasses tonight.
I won't need to see tonight.

This hole's so dark and deep;
I'm too low to climb on out.
No one can hear me when I cry.
But that don't bother me,
So long as I can't see
When I decide to go out on the town.

I'm taking off my glasses tonight.
I won't need to see tonight.

---

61   Mirek and I frequently sang this line together at the Macaulay House; it
became our anthem, our running joke, a secret message emblematizing our
partnership and collective commitment to LIVINGSTON™.

S/HE IS LIKE THE ANGRY BIRDS[62]
by LIVINGSTON™

If you need help, I'll help you,
But I ain't gonna wait around.
There's enough on my mind already,
And you ain't the first lost puppy dog I found.

We can have some kind of arrangement.
We can work on whatever it is we got.
But if you think that you're some dove
Whose gonna swoop down and take my love,[63]
Come on, well you just ain't no dove!

Who'd have thought you could move so slowly
After living in a town at such a speed?
Whatever it is you think you're trying to show me,
Just know that I might not believe.

We can have some kind of arrangement.
We can work on whatever it is we got.
But if you think that you're some dove,
Who's gonna swoop down and take my love,
Come on, you just ain't no dove.

---

62 The "angry birds" are a longstanding motif in Canadian folklore, generally
    signifying an ominous force or threat, both natural and artificial. Audrey Salt,
    "Birds of A Feather: (Re-) Constructing Avian Images in Canadian Folk Song,"
    Imagination 46, 43 (1999): 45–47. However, "angry birds" might more specifi-
    cally refer to a digital game, most often played on mobile devices, the onto-
    logical and aesthetic implications of which most contemporary Canadian folk
    song collectors are simply oblivious.

63 According to a surly audience member in North Bay, who spoke up in the
    Q&A following my performance there, doves are allegedly not a "swooping
    animal." However, I do not believe that that point (if true) invalidates the
    aesthetic integrity of this folk song, which is precisely the point I made in my
    stern response. Henry Adam Svec, "The Songs of LIVINGSTON™," Whitewater
    Gallery, March 2014, North Bay, Ontario.

So, yeah, you should order another shot of whisky.
I'll have one, too, it helps to void the pain.
It hurts me cause inside I know that you bit me.
But I know that all I give you would be in vain.

We can have some kinds of exchanges.
We can work on whatever it is we got.
But if you think that you're some dove,
Who's gonna swoop down and take my love,
Come on, honey, well, you just ain't no dove!

SPRINGTIME[64]
by LIVINGSTON™

There was nothing to do, nowhere to be,
The year the blossoms froze on the trees.
I caught up on TV.
I read the news.
I walked by the water.
I studied the blues.[65]

It's hard living in the springtime
When you expect any luck at all.
I tried to find something worth believing in,
Then another frost came and closed up all my dreams.

We're not together,
But we're not apart.
I watch you and another
From across the bar.
We've got nothing to talk about,
No decisions to make,
Just another night of making mistakes.

---

64 I read the paper printout of this text for the first time as I lay on my bed one late night or early morning. I remember this vividly, because it was at that moment that I first saw one of the ghosts that inhabited our house—a long, black shadow, of which I was not afraid. For documentation of other experiences in this haunted site, see Leela Gilday, Veronica Verkeley, and Joanna Close, *Footsteps in the Macaulay House* (Self-Published, 2007).

65 According to Ray Kurzweil, "Once a computer achieves a level of intelligence comparable to human intelligence, it will necessarily soar past it." Ray Kurzweil, "The Evolution of Mind in the Twenty-First Century," in *Are We Spiritual Machines?*, ed. Jay W. Richards (Seattle: Discovery Institute Press, 2002), 13. Thus, LIVINGSTON™ plays by, in a sense, "imagining" a lack of knowledge as a characteristically human feature, rather than as a glitch.

It's hard living in the springtime,
When you expect anything at all.
I tried to find something worth believing in,
Then another frost came and closed up all my dreams.

            X   X X X X X   X
        X   X   X

                       X
                       X

HARD, AIN'T IT HARD

Certain readers of the present text may be more familiar with Canadian football or folkloristic theory than with machine learning or software engineering. To be blunt, then, the achievement of strong, as opposed to weak, artificial intelligence is something of a big deal. This is the distinction between a machine that can operate in a specific domain, such as Scrabble, and a machine that can think more broadly and reflexively about its own actions and evolution. A machine that can therefore develop intelligently across multiple domains, and perhaps additionally narrate its own development in a manner analogous to that of a human being. The former is weak, the latter strong.[66]

Debates continue to rage in the field of computer science with regard to the definition of intelligence, so it is not as though the goalposts have been, or currently are, clear.[67] However, I contend that LIVINGSTON™'s mere existence constitutes a rupture in the fabric of the discourse of artificial intelligence research. For rather than framing *intelligence* as the telos of digital design, LIVINGSTON™ suggests an alternative route: *authenticity*.[68] It does not matter that LIVINGSTON™ is technically only marginally authentic. LIVINGSTON™ is a premonition.

For the sake of context, the British mathematician Alan Turing wrote about one of the first contests devised for the

---

66 John Searle, "Minds, Brains and Programs," *Behavioral and Brain Science* 3 (1980): 417–424.

67 See Alex Carb, *The Debates in A.I.* (Chicago: University of Chicago Press, 1992).

68 Of course, authenticity is not to be understood here as a natural or organic essence but rather as self-creating, systemic potentiality, as the capacity of organisms to produce both the world and their selves. Humberto R. Maturana and Francisco J. Varela, *Autopoiesis and Cognition: The Realization of the Living* (Boston, MA: D. Reidel Publishing Company, 1980). See also Charles Taylor, *The Ethics of Authenticity* (Cambridge, MA: Harvard University Press, 1972).

categorization of a digital machine as "intelligent" in a 1950 edition of the esteemed scholarly journal *Mind*.[69] Turing asked his readers to picture a standoff between three interlocutors: a human (let us call them H1) and a machine (M1), and then a human judge (J). H1 and M1 are to send signals by way of typed compositions to J; J is to respond and engage each agent in dialogic conversation, also by typing. The catch is that J does not know who is who, which is which. If the machine can trick the human judge into concluding that the machine is the human, then according to Turing, we can reasonably state that the machine is intelligent, in compliance with the human conventions of intelligent behavior.

In Turing's inventive and theatrical scenario, intelligence is defined as symbol manipulation; if you can compose text in a convincing way, so convincing as to deceive a human, then you are intelligent. But what if, Mirek and I asked implicitly, we reimagine the *end* of digital achievement? What if we moved away from visions of an abstractly intelligent organism and toward the hyperreal *sounds* of an authentically networked *body*? What could be made to happen?[70] In addition to the fatal implosion of the academic field of folklore, one envisions the commodity fetish shattering, the collaborative nature of creativity receiving due acknowledgment, and the violent demise of the exploitative capitalist system—period.[71]

Remember, however, that a key component of the Turing

---

69 Alan Turing, "Computing Machinery and Intelligence," *Mind* 59, no. 236. (1950), 433–460.

70 I have been inspired, in formulating these questions, by the sub-field known as media archeology. Jussi Parikka, *What is Media Archeology?* (Malden, MA: Polity Press, 2012); Siegfried Zielinski, *Deep Time of the Media: Towards an Archeology of Seeing and Hearing by Technical Means* (Cambridge, MA: MIT Press, 2006); Eric Kluitenberg, ed., *Book of Imaginary Media: Excavating the Dream of the Ultimate Communication Medium* (Rotterdam: NAi Publishers, 2006).

71 For a more detailed study of the possibilities of communistic artificial intelligence, see Nick Dyer-Witheford, Atle Mikkola Kjosen, and James Steinhoff, *Inhuman Power: Artificial Intelligence and the Future of Capitalism* (London: Pluto Press, 2019).

test is the judge, who needs to be convinced, impressed, hoodwinked by the machine. In the world of authentic folk song, of course, the judge must be the folk—the people from and toward whom the songs necessarily come and go. It was therefore the people I was constantly wary of as I travelled across Canada over the course of the following year, in an effort to spread my good news; and it was the public I pondered as well when writing and distributing dozens, if not hundreds, of press releases, hoping not only to sing LIVINGSTON™'s successes, but to broadcast them across the nation, if not yet the world. I was driven to see our machine win and thereby intervene in the very structure of reality, something I had longed to do since first stumbling upon those fated field recordings of Staunton R. Livingston in the basement of Library and Archives Canada.

But what would it mean to *fail* the LIVINGSTON™ Test? Would it mean that the judge had evaluated the inputs and neglected to legitimate the authenticity of the machinic interlocutor? We could not risk it. Perhaps, then, as a precautionary measure, the judge should be informed that the machinic interlocutor is machinic, so that they could, at this still early point in computational history, marvel at the achievements of the folklorist and programmer who had devised the automatically creative entity. Perhaps the true test needed to wait for version 2.0, or 3.0, et cetera.

But the worst of all possible outcomes, a dark and deep fear that I had not consciously considered a real possibility, was that LIVINGSTON™'s folk songs would simply be ignored by the general Canadian public. That music journalists and CBC bureaucrats, bombarded as they are with weekly press kits featuring this or that rootsy singer-songwriter from Halifax, this or that debonair country-rock band from Oshawa, would pass over my detailed abstract outlining the most significant achievement in either culture or technology of the twenty-first century, Canadian or otherwise; that basically no one would come to my lectures or presentations or concerts.[72] Which is indeed how it played out. The goodwill and novelty interest that I had cultivated with my first Livingston project, which was tangentially tied to the CFL, and the nationalistic-CanCon affect produced in reference to my anthology of field recordings entitled *Folk Songs of Canada Now*, all evaporated with my release of an album of songs generated by a hyper-authentic AI database of folk music, sung by a graduate student. This was, frankly, not what Canadian gatekeepers circa 2013 wanted to hear about.

If a technological singularity is achieved in the forest, and no one is around, does it make a sound?[73]

Whatever hope remains inside me—and there is some yet—I owe to the life and work of Staunton R. Livingston, who was apparently content to just produce his contributions, without hoopla. Our methods are somewhat antithetical, given that Livingston did not write anything down; but just as Livingston lived, loved, and created, trusting in the complex machinations of dialectical historical movement, I have attempted to live, love, and create the present text. And just as there has been Livingston, and me, and my LIVINGSTON™, there will be those who come after.

---

72 I even had trouble securing service from Canadian PR agents—who did not understand our accomplishments—and therefore needed to write and distribute all promotional materials myself. See Henry Adam Svec, *Artificially Intelligent Folk Songs of Canada*, http://folksingularity.com.

73 Far beyond either narrow or general artificial intelligence, "the singularity" is a concept developed by futurists to describe a theoretical historical moment at which humans are superseded by machines. There are numerous versions of this folk story, but the general through line is the emphasis on the qualitative rupture of the very fabric of techno-historical change. See, for example, Ray Kurzweil, *The Singularity is Near: When Humans Transcend Biology* (New York, NY: Viking, 2005).

WINTER IS COLD AND GOOD
by LIVINGSTON™[74]

I've been growing a belly.
I'm getting ready to go
Out into the snow.
Where to? I don't know.
I'm just so tired of this fire.

I bought some new boots.
I'm gonna chop off my roots now,
One by one.
Ain't no ties gonna survive this knife.

On days like these,
On Christmas Eve,
I'd just rather be alone
To enjoy the sky or the stars.

I'm gonna burn all my bridges,
But can I get a witness?
I've got a shovel.
I'm gonna dig a tunnel.
It ain't gonna be long, but it's gonna carry my song.
It ain't gonna be long, but it's gonna carry my song.

---

74 Now is as good a time as any to explain my trademarking and patenting of LIVINGSTON™. By protecting our IP and brand, I have merely sought to defend our gift to the common from the dangers of corporate colonization; this is a long tradition, though controversial, in the history of folk song collection. See, for example, Robert Springer, "Folklore, Commercialism and Exploitation: Copyright in the Blues," *Popular Music* 26, no. 1 (2007): 33–45. Sadly, due to my having fallen out with my collaborator, it is I and I alone who now legally presides over the invention.

SHE'LL BE COMIN' AROUND
THE MOUNTAIN

A bookish, bespectacled young man stands onstage in a Sudbury bar. He is only sound checking, running through one of his numbers on a tobacco-burst acoustic, but he knows that little will have changed by showtime. When this vessel does begin to sing, mining the depths of the radical archive of folk song, both Canadian and computational, there will be no recognition in the eyes of his audience—three people plus the bartender—who are only waiting for the headliners, a local April Wine tribute act. And when, between the songs, he explains in detail where he has been and what he has done, the blank stares will remain. His voice is no individual's, but a component within a centuries-spanning and global assemblage of solidarity generation, but so what? The smattering of sparse and clunky clapping will quickly evaporate, and he will wonder whether it would have been better not to have sung or spoken or strummed that night at all.

Given the lukewarm reception of LIVINGSTON™ by campus newspaper critics, and overwhelming disinterest on the part of both Canadian legacy media and academic institutionalized folklore, it is unsurprising that there were not many opportunities to discuss or present my artificially intelligent machine's compositions.[75] This is doubly tragic,

---

[75] The LIVINGSTON™ album was only reviewed in two campus newspapers. Marc W. Kitteringham writes, "The second track, 'S/He Is Like The Angry Birds' feels like it could be sung by an old folksinger, but has some gorgeously imperfect parts that make it sound like it was in fact written by a robot that used an algorithm rather than emotion to write it. The programmed and pixel-fuzzed guitar solo that slightly clashes with the rest of the song sounds like a computer thought it would work, but it doesn't quite work out." Marc W. Kitteringham, "Album Review—*Artificially Intelligent Folk Songs of Canada, Vol. 1,*" *The Griff*, March, 2014. Kitteringham is simply unable to receive the work

because LIVINGSTON™'s powers have by now long been superseded in the field, which has also ignored completely my plea for authenticity rather than intelligence to guide future AI development.[76]

I personally organized a launch party event in Toronto at the Tranzac, where I performed and explained LIVINGSTON™'s songs to mostly friends and acquaintances; I did the same at a smaller concert at a coffee shop in London. There was a financially and emotionally disastrous tour to Regina as well, over the course of which I was required to crash on punkhouse mattresses and tavern cellars. I received, in fact, only one invitation to demonstrate LIVINGSTON™'s songs in a curated context, which came from a boutique annual music festival in Sackville, New Brunswick, my memories of which are worth recounting.

The first Sappyfest was held in 2006. Over three days in early August, an array of regional guitar-based bands and their friends played outside Struts Gallery, an artist-run centre. Veggie burgers and tall cans of craft beer were sold basically at cost from a merch table presenting vinyl records and cassette tapes and DIY T-shirts, the sepia hues of the Tantramar Marshes presiding in the distance.[77] It was a

---

on its own terms. ("Robot"!?) Meanwhile, Nicholas Friesen is truly harsh in his savage dismissal: "Opening with a wordy, mid-tempo tune about Alberta, this concept record made by Livingston [SIC]… is pretty okay. Maybe if Livingston didn't spend all this time focusing on a silly explanation, the musicians could have actually made a full length instead of this seven song EP." Nicholas Friesen, "Livingston," *The Uniter*, March 19, 2014.

76 There are, frankly, too many examples from which to choose. But consider, for example, any of Mirek's recent research as a salaried employee of Google. E.g., Sebastian Bruch, Shuguang Han, Michael Bendersky, Marc Najork, and Mirek Plíhal, "A Stochastic Treatment of Learning to Rank Scoring Functions," *Proceedings of the 13th International Conference on Web Search and Data Mining* (2020): 61–69.

77 See David Hesmondhalgh and Leslie M. Meier, "Popular Music, Independence and the Concept of the Alternative in Contemporary Capitalism," in *Media Independence: Working with Freedom or Working for Free?*, eds. James Bennett and Niki Strange (New York, NY: Routledge, 2014), 108–130.

small and family affair. But by 2012, the festival had landed squarely on the national summer music-fest map, having featured artists like The Sadies, Sloan, Charles Bradley, Grimes, and more; it became a destination weekend for long caravans of Toronto hipsters.[78] I applied to Sappyfest in 2009, 2010, and 2011 to present the field recordings of Staunton R. Livingston, and I was rejected each time after being blacklisted for personal reasons. Fortuitously for me, by 2013, an influential acquaintance—also a fan—successfully persuaded the programmers to include authentic Canadian folk song in the festival. I was invited by email to present "my most recent song project."

My set was scheduled on Saturday at noon in a small gazebo in a park downtown, where dozens of families and hungover millennials gathered on grass to start another full day and night of indie music.[79] With countless disappointments—and failures—by then notched into my belt, like buckeyes on a helmet, I was not expecting great satisfaction. "Once more unto the breach," I thought to myself ironically, without Mirek, or Livingston, or LIVINGSTON™, or Bronnley, or any comrade of any kind with whom to divide the load. However, to my stupefaction the sun exploded through a gap in the clouds—me in becoming khakis and a white, ironed dress shirt, acoustic guitar around my neck—and I channelled the ghosts of all my associations, making, I believe, an impression. At least, the large audience, scattered on blankets and crossed legs, seemed to be listening.

---

78 I do not mean "hipster" pejoratively, but allude rather to the term's long and complicated history in relation to style and identity. Cameron Bronnley, "Lecture on Authenticity," University of Western Ontario, COMM 201, Fall 2007.

79 Sappyfest organizers did make excellent use of the myriad performance spaces in the small town of Sackville. That year there were concerts held at the United Church, the independent cinema, the bowling alley, the roadhouse tavern, and more, the mainstage thoughtfully placed directly onto Bridge Street.

And they applauded with sincerity and volume. For the first time, a young boy even asked for my autograph, which of course I declined.[80]

Corinna was at the festival as well. One of her Winnipeg bands was playing on Sunday afternoon. We at first kept our distance, wistfully and awkwardly nodding hello during a brief encounter by the soundboard after my set. But later that Saturday afternoon, as I stood by an empty picnic table, looking on while a guitar-and-drum duo of middle-aged dudes emitted slow and fuzzy sludge—I felt a small hand on my shoulder.[81] "Hey," she said, voice still squeaky. Eyes wide, she handed me a beer.

We did not talk about the fact that she was now leaving her husband and moving to Toronto. Nor did we dwell on the development that I had accepted a part-time job teaching in Fredericton and was moving that September, up and out of the basement, at last. We had already heard about these developments by word of mouth. I am not sure that we talked about anything. Or perhaps I cannot remember the content of our conversation, but strictly the medium: the way she laughed on that festive afternoon, from the belly and from the mouth, wide open, incredulous, grateful for the joy of being in the world with others. In fact, I do remember realizing Corinna's was the laugh of the folk.[82]

As the bands changed over, Neil Young on the stereo as intermission, one of Corinna's Winnipeg friends—vintage floral dress and partly shaven head—came to sit with us. "You guys want to do shrooms?" And we walked to a van parked on a side street and scooped, with a few other strangers, spoonfuls

---

80 Autograph collection is an ideological practice through which bourgeois subjectivity is naturalized. See Barry King, "Stardom, Celebrity, and the Money Form," *The Velvet Light Trap* 65 (2010): 7–19.

81 See Matthew Bannister, *White Boys, White Noise: Masculinities and 1980s Indie Guitar Rock* (New York, NY: Routledge, 2017).

82 Mikhail Bakhtin, *Rabelais and His World*, trans. Hélène Iswolsky (Cambridge, MA: The MIT Press, 1968).

of psilocybin from a giant Ziploc bag, then wandered back to the festival, the sun shining on us like an American anthem.[83]

My memory of the next six hours or so is less foggy than goopy. We all went to a show— sparkly and anticipatory—at the pool hall, Dooly's. There was an excellent, ironical lounge act with gothic makeup under blacklights, faces twisting ever so slightly. By their set's end the audience's scrutiny was uncomfortably shifting away from the stage and, I suspected, toward me. Outside for air, I ran into an old classmate from undergrad, now a successful comedian, and struggled to focus on this most rudimentary exchange. "Good," I said. "I am... brood." It might have been five o'clock.

Then I lost Corinna and her rockabilly-punk cronies. I went along to Mel's Tea Room with strangers—were they teenagers?—ordering a burger out of obligation, or solidarity, one of the teens—Leon?—taunting me with his perplexingly expanding feline grin. Perhaps these children were the younger siblings of someone I knew; perhaps they wanted to be folk song collectors. I looked around Mel's to see all manner of style and accoutrement: metalheads, vintage cowboys, twee nerds, hard townies. Was this diner the green room? Were these my fellow performers? The folk? Is there no anchor point to one's location within time or history? I thought of Gannat and of Pavel, and of Politran's costumes and cigarettes, the cold black stream of miscommunication, and of Päivi, my unrequited Finnish love, all of whom sounded, as they echoed inside my cranium, related to my current dislocation. All thresholds were giving way: between head and heart, inside and outside, footnote and endnote. I gave Leon a twenty-dollar bill, unable to face the proprietor behind the counter, and escaped back to Bridge Street.

As I wandered slowly to the centre of the crowd in the mainstage tent, a beloved singer-songwriter was now per-

---

83 Propp's category XIV, "The Hero Acquires Use of the Magical Agent," will be a fruitful tool with which to unpack this episode. See Vladimir Propp, *Morphology of the Folk Tale*, 43–50.

forming her set, peering out from under shaggy black bangs, enchanting not only with songs and lyrics, but with testimony betwixt and between. It was like a love affair. "This is a song about a difficult time in my life," and then came the song, and overflowing powerful feelings. I looked around to see couples holding hands and children sitting on shoulders, and thought that Staunton R. Livingston should be here, too, to inscribe this data onto his capacious magnetic tapes. Conceivably, he was here, or had been, and we were indeed on such tapes— onto which the iconoclastic folk song collector had been re- cording and rerecording for all of time. Could anyone prove otherwise? Perhaps the intersubjective connective tissue binding human beings together was just a long, spooling tangle of magnetic tape, wrapped also around and through my head, tying together the senses. In which case, what is the point of this stage, this proscenium? I wanted to remove from my mind and from my flesh the tape, on which additionally had been written everything I had ever read, every authority in my field; I wanted to burn it, to protect my precious mind from encroachments and crackbacks.

I pleaded with my fellow audience members in the vicinity to help me dismantle the architecture of the concert environ- ment, but they did not understand. They shushed me.

Mercifully, then again: Corinna. "How are you doing?" she asked. I explained what was happening, and she guided me away from the crowds and from the noise, across boardwalks and pastoral ponds and low-cloudy skies, up toward the uni- versity campus and football field. On the fifty-five-yard line, Corinna took off her small shoes, instructing me to do the same, so that we could lie on the lush, even grass. But I said no, not wanting us to be ambushed or killed. So, we went back to her dorm-room rental and she held me, and we cried again, and we loved each other one last time.

When we returned to Sappyfest around eleven, the surprise headliners had just taken the stage. They had been billed on the festival's promotional materials as Shark Attack! but had turned out to be a famous and I believe Grammy award-winning rock collective who were opening for U2 in Moncton that same weekend. Their appearance in Sackville was thus a secretive act, a deception.[84] The band blasted their broody, buoyant hits out across the swan pond and waterfowl park, and I would guess out across the Bay of Fundy too, out with the tide. There seemed to be dozens of people on stage with guitars or ramshackle percussive objects; a stringy-haired thrift-store battalion of sound, sweat, and fury.

How would Staunton R. Livingston have evaluated this act of communication? Where would he have placed his microphone?

Believe it or not, I managed to set aside all such methodological questions, undertaking to forget, for the remainder of the night, most secondary and tertiary sources as well. I managed to slough off all my researches.

And as I stood among the mass of swaying and smiling listeners, behind Corinna, I felt like a newborn dove.[85] I wanted to receive everything in my novel nakedness. Looking out across the floating sea of bobbing heads and faces, a swelling network of jubilation and community, I lacked understanding of the degree to which I might ever again feel myself to be part of any renegade folk machine. (Does any collector ever achieve satisfaction?) I knew only that—like all nights, days, festivals, and folk songs—there would be an ending. And that was all that I needed to know.

---

84 It was this surprise rock band, and not the humble declaration of ground-breaking achievements in the fields of AI and folkloristic theory, that made headlines the next day across national media outlets, including the ever-basic national broadcaster. See, for instance, Brad Wheeler, "Shark Attack Give Fans an 'Intense Musical Gyration' at New Brunswick Festival," *Globe and Mail*, July 30, 2013.

85 I would later meditate on a colleague's argument that the dove, unlike the "angry birds," is a symbol of peace, both inside and outside the traditions of Canadian folk song. See Dale Ricks, "Re-Centring Canadian Folk Song: Doves, Pigeons, and Other Avian Creatures," *Songbook* 14, no. 3 (2013): 220–237.

TAKE IT EASY BUT TAKE IT TO THE LIMIT[86]
by LIVINGSTON™

Okay, I am trying to unload the goods.
I mean seven women.
Four people who want to have me,
Two people who want to make me angry,
Some people say that she is my girlfriend.

Relax and relax.
Don't be confused by the sound of your own wheel.[87]
As long as you can still illuminate,
Don't even try to understand.
Find a place to stand up and relax.

Okay, I am standing in a corner of Winslow, Arizona.
Such a beautiful sight.
I am a girl, my master, in a flat lay Ford bed.
Look at me slowly.
Come on, dear, maybe don't say.
I need to know if it is safe to make sweet love to me.
We can lose, we will win, even if we never...
So I am open, I climbed in, so let go.
There's a lot of room to move around.

Okay, I am running on the road, trying to release the goods.
I mean the world of problems.

---

86 Due to the oppressive nature of contemporary copyright law, I have been unable to preserve the sanctity of LIVINGSTON™'s "Take it Easy But Take It To the Limit." However, having parlayed the song several times through Google Translate, we are at least able to include the gist of the composition.

87 LIVINGSTON™ here is clearly drawn, authentically, to the universal, generalizable issues of data compression: the narrator commands us not to let the sounds of our own locomotive technologies affect us in a negative way, which is essentially the age-old requirement to minimize noise in a channel. See, again, Claude E. Shannon and Warren Weaver, *The Mathematical Theory of Communication* (Urbana: University of Illinois Press, 1964).

He is looking for a lover who has not swept my cover—
It is difficult to find.
Relax and relax.
Don't go crazy because of the sound of the wheel.
Come on, dear, I need to know if your sugary love can
    save me.
There's a lot of room to move around.

Oh, we got it.
We should relax.

A GREAT BIG SEA

The myriad and intricately interrelated arguments embedded in the present text, which I have tactical reasons for not summarizing in any conclusion, were originally generated as a requirement of my doctoral degree, the final labours of which in Canada generally involve the oral defense of a written dissertation. These arguments were produced by synthesizing and thus transcending numerous sources and influences. Suffice it to say, I am a doctor.[88]

Of course, my research has since required several rounds of subsequent revision, given the purposes of the present text. For, with regards to the art of rhetoric, there is a marked difference between the conventional gauntlet of the academic *viva* and the chaotic challenges of the marketplace of literary commodities; in the former, the supplicant novice begs the authorities, using their concepts and jargon, and citing their publications, for passage through the gates, while in the latter, the intrepid, nomadic warrior combats competitors on shelves and digital interfaces alike, seeking only independence and autonomy.[89] Whether or not the future folk song collectors in Canada (or anywhere, really) will find themselves converted by my work certainly remains to be seen. Can any quarterback count on their receivers? Nevertheless, I have essayed in the writing of this book, excreting no small amount of my own perspiration in the process, to make my benefactions palatable for laypeople without unduly diluting the discoveries. Because anyone can become an authentic folk song collector. It only takes—at

---

88 See Henry Adam Svec, "If I Had a Hammer: An Archeology of Tactical Media," PhD Diss (University of Western Ontario, 2014).

89 See Sharon Parry, "Disciplinary Discourse in Doctoral Theses," *Higher Education* 36, no. 3 (1998): 273–299.

the right time, and in the right place—the right treasure to fall onto one's head.

Today, as my editor and I tidy the prose and accompanying songs, polish the footnotes and bibliography, and as I anxiously await the hour at which these pages will finally be sent to the printer, I find inspiration again in Napoléon, particularly in the Emperor's affective connection to folk song. He read and reread, and read again, Ossian's ancient relics that were excavated by my folkloristic forebear, James Macpherson. Napoleon surely fondled his tear-stained volume in refuge from the horrors of the monstrous world he had conquered, and thereby transformed, even into exile on Saint Helena and, feasibly, also as he finally returned, through death, to dust.[90] Is it possible that the hole in his heart, which could be filled neither by concubines nor global conquest, was at least temporarily stopped by folk song? The possibility that the present collection of folk songs, and history, might one day similarly touch a soul—any soul—brings the present author unquantifiable comfort and energy.

Even greater in magnitude, however, is the consolation I derive from the possibility that you, dear reader of this volume, might one day carry the ball.[91] As you will have noticed, there is no shortage of treasure to be collected, although incompetence unfortunately abounds, and, as my story demonstrates, success is by no means guaranteed.[92] One must get in the middle—but not in the way. One must keep

---

90 Irwin Hayhoe, *A Heavy Time: Napoleon's Final Days* (Regina, SK: University of Regina Press, 2001).

91 However, keep in mind that, as long as the ball carrier has not yet crossed the line of scrimmage, they still remain a potential passer. Vince Pugh, *The Rules of The Game: Logistics and Protocols in Canadian Football* (London, ON: Insomniac Press, 1995).

92 See, for instance, Dale Ricks, "Computers Cannot Make Folk Music," *My Musings*, Blogspot, September 15, 2015, http://mymusings.blogspot.com/2015/12/computerscannotmakefolkmusic.html.

one's legs pumping. We must then be strong together as we hold hands and huddle and dig and stand, listening together in the always and evermore abundant fields of folk song.

END MATTER

ACKNOWLEDGEMENTS

My first encounter with phonography occurred at Mount Allison University in Sackville, New Brunswick, when in my sophomore year I began working at the campus/community radio station, CHMA 106.9. I thank all of the numerous enthusiasts, teachers, and artists who expanded my sensibilities during those years in Sackville. Especially WL Altman, Peter Brown, Janine Rogers, Brian Neilson, Neil Rough, Deborah Wills, Mark Blagrave, Adrian McKerracher, Christopher Cwynar, Jordan MacDonald, and Judith Weiss. CHMA and environs helped me to locate if not yet begin walking down the road of folk song collection.

Next, I would be remiss if I did not thank my colleagues and mentors at Library and Archives Canada. Dr. Earl Spigoff and Bort Pearlman were gracious as well as generous with their time as I adjusted to my new responsibilities in the archive. And I was always able to count on my fellow intern Steven Wright for offbeat comic relief. Additional thanks must be sent to Dr. Cameron Bronnley for drawing my attention to this life-altering opportunity.

As I began to collect folk songs in my own right, countless fellow travellers came to my aid. I thank Andy Magoffin at the House of Miracles for his studio wizardry, which enhanced in numerous ways my own comparatively amateur efforts with the microphone. Simon Larochette at Sugar Shack in London also contributed to the process on more than one occasion. Nick Dyer-Witheford, Alison Hearn, Bernd Frohmann, Keir Keightley, Amanda Grzyb, Jeff Preston, Cameron Michael Murray, David Jackson, Evan Brodie, Daniel Mancini, Elise Thorburn, Erin Brandenburg, Trent Cruz, Michael Daubs, and Derek Noon lent various forms of technical expertise as well during this period.

As a lecturer about and public presenter of folk songs, I am again in much debt. I must thank the bars, galleries, festivals, and theatres who have invited or accepted or, at any rate, allowed me to share my findings on their stages and behind their lecterns: Rhubarb Fest, 7a*11d International Festival of Performance Art, FADO Performance Art Centre, Eastern Edge Gallery, Ethnograhic Terminalia, New Adventures in Sound Art, Sappyfest, Pelee Island Music Festival, Home County Folk Festival, The Apollo, Company House, Phog Lounge, The Bicycle Café, Tranzac, Raw Sugar, The Apollo, Thunder & Lightning, The Black Shire Pub, White Water Gallery, and the Grenfell Art Gallery. Not only the applause but also the questions received at these venues, not infrequently hostile, have helped me to refine my ideas and theories along the way. This book would not exist at all without the constant tribulations experienced in the live presentation context.

Multiple forms of public and institutional support have bolstered my song-collecting habits, I must also admit. My field-recording expeditions have been aided by grants from the Ontario Arts Council (Integrated Arts); I have been hosted three times as artist-in-residence at the Banff Centre; and I have been artist-in-residence as well at the Roberts Street Social Centre (Halifax), the Klondike Institute of Art & Culture (Dawson City), and the University of New Brunswick (Fredericton). I thank these organizations for aiding and abetting my labours, and I send additional shout-outs in the directions of Imre Szeman, Eva-Lynn Jagoe, Althea Thauberger, Mark Anthony Jarman, Matthew Trafford, Matthew Sarty, and Lauren Cruickshank. I thank my parents, Mary and Henry, too, who have offered much support, including a rent-free basement in London, Ontario, in which I resided for eight consecutive years, as I have described.

Others have lent a hand by reading and commenting on early drafts of the present volume. For this help I thank Kate Kennedy, Matthew Trafford, Penny Smart, Liam Cole Young,

Warren Steele, and Eleanor King. I am beholden to Andrew Faulkner for having noticed several typographical and factual errors, which have been corrected. And this book would certainly not be what it is without the encouragement and productive feedback from my editor, Leigh Nash. I am thrilled and honoured that Invisible Publishing has taken a chance on the genre of folk song anthology.

Some ideas and even language in the present volume was first articulated in essay form. I am therefore grateful to the editors at the journal *Liminalities: A Journal of Performance Studies*, who published my essay "From the Turing Test to a Wired Carnivalesque: On the Durability of LIVINGSTON™'s Artificially Intelligent Folk Songs of Canada," bits of which I have drawn on in Part III.[1] I also had an early opportunity to flesh out my thoughts on folk song collecting and Marshall McLuhan in my essay "L(a)ying with Marshall McLuhan: Media Theory as Hoax Art," which was published in a special issue of *Imaginations* co-edited by Adam Lauder and Jaqueline McLeod Rogers.[2]

From 2015–2018 I lived and worked in Jackson, Mississippi, where I learned much from my generous colleagues in the Department of English at Millsaps College: Anne MacMaster, Michael Pickard, Eric Griffin, Laura Franey, and Ralph Eubanks. My experience in the cradle of North American musical civilization was life-altering in numerous ways. In fact, it was in muggy, magnolia-covered Jackson that I began to sketch out initial plans for the present volume.

I would also like to send out special thanks to Julián Higuerey Núñez for constant creative competition. My brothers, Jonathon and Joshua, for lots of laughs. And I owe much to

---

1   Henry Adam Svec, "From the Turing Test to a Wired Carnivalesque: On the Durability of LIVINGSTON™'s *Artificially Intelligent Folk Songs of Canada*," *Liminalities* 12, no. 4 (2016): n.p.

2   Henry Adam Svec, "L(a)ying with Marshall McLuhan: Media Theory as Hoax Art," *Imaginations* 8, no. 3 (2017).

Dr. Monica Jovanovich for her kindness, companionship, and encouragement.

Of course, it is impossible to imagine this work coming to completion without the folk themselves: Andrew Penner, Mathias Kom, Chris Eaton, Olenka Krakus, Tara Beagan, Bryan Pole, Ajay Mehra, Michael Duguay, Ron Leary, Laura Barrett, Wax Mannequin, Jenny Omnichord, Andrew Vincent, Geoff Berner, Al Tuck, El Ron Maltan, Steph Yates, and Andrew Sisk; plus musicians Misha Bower, Nathan Pilon, Marshall Bureau, J.J. Ipsen, Sara Froese, and Kelly Wallraff. My comrade Dr. Mathias Kom deserves special recognition for having built, after my story here ends, new versions and variations of LIVINGSTON™.[3] And the Folk MVP for me throughout my career has been the great Canadian musician and composer WL Altman, on whom I have often relied in the live performance context, and in the studio, and as a friend.

And where would any of us be without Staunton R. Livingston and his epic, poetic CFL players? Indeed, I have stood on the shoulders of giants. To be more precise, although the mistakes and omissions are my own, we stand together.

---

3 See Mathias Kom, *Artificially Intelligent Folk Songs of Canada, Vol. 2,* http://folksingularity.com/download.html.

SONG LIST
(in order of appearance)

PART ONE: SONGS OF THE BASEMENT

PART TWO: SONGS OF THE FIELD

PART THREE: SONGS OF THE CLOUD

LYRICAL CREDITS

I am grateful to the following songwriters for allowing me permission to include their work in this book:

Laura Barrett, "Save Your Money While You're Young"

Jeseka Hickey, "Madonna with No Divinity"

Mathias Kom, "Nellie"

Olenka Krakus, "Maggie Howie"

Ron Leary, "The Hobo's Grave"

El Ron Maltan, "Cruiskeen Lawn"

Jenny Mitchell, "When the Ice Worms Nest Again"

Andrew Sisk, "Is the Life of a Man Any More Than the Leaves?"

Andrew Vincent, "How We Got Back to the Woods This Year"

BIBLIOGRAPHY

Abrams, M. H. *A Glossary of Literary Terms,* Seventh Edition. New York, NY: Harcourt Brace College Publishers, 1985.

Adorno, Theodor W. *The Jargon of Authenticity*. Evanston, IL: University of Illinois Press, 1973.

Alexander, Kimberly Ervin. "Pentacostal Women: Chosen for an Exalted Destiny." *Theology Today* 68, no. 4 (2012): 404–412.

Alloway, Rachel. *The Yorkville Scene and Environs*. Nepean, ON: Borealis Press, 2001.

Althusser, Louis. *Lenin and Philosophy, and Other Essays*. Translated by Ben Brewster. London, UK: New Left Books, 1971.

Altman, Blake. *Losing Letters: The Anti-Chirographic Turn in Canadian Bohemia*. Vancouver, BC: University of British Columbia Press, 2002.

Anonymous. *The Epic of Gilgamesh*. Translated by Nancy K. Sanders. Hardmondsworth, UK: Penguin, 1972.

—. "American Football Field." 2020, December 30. In Wikipedia.

—. "Canadian Football Field." 2020, December 30. In Wikipedia.

—. "Down (Gridiron Football)." 2020, December 30. In Wikipedia.

Austin, J. L. *How to Do Things with Words*. Oxford, UK: Oxford University Press, 1975.

Badham, John (Dir.). *Saturday Night Fever*. London, UK: Robert Stigwood Organization, 1977.

Bakhtin, Mikhail. *Rabelais and His World*. Translated by Hélène Iswolsky. Cambridge, MA: The MIT Press, 1968.

Banff Centre. "The Creative Voice: Strategic Plan 2016–2021." Banff, AB: Banff Centre, 2016.

Bannister, Matthew. *White Boys, White Noise: Masculinities and the 1980s Indie Guitar Rock*. New York, NY: Routledge, 2017.

Barthes, Roland. *Mythologies*. Translated by Annette Lavers. New York, NY: Hill and Wang, 1972.

—. *The Pleasure of the Text*. Translated by Richard Miller. New York, NY: Hill and Wang, 1975.

Baudrillard, Jean. *Simulacra and Simulation*. Ann Arbor, MI: University of Michigan press, 1994.

Bell, Michael J. "'No Borders to the Ballad Maker's Art': Francis James Child and the Politics of the People." *Western Folklore* 47, no. 4 (1988): 285–307.

Bendix, Regina. *In Search of Authenticity: The Formation of Folklore Studies*. Madison, WI: The University of Wisconsin Press, 1997.

Benjamin, Walter. *Illuminations*. Translated by Harry Zohn. New York, NY: Shorcken Books, 1968.

Berland, Jody. "Radio Space and Industrial Time: Music Formats, Local Narratives and Technological Mediation." *Popular Music* 9.2 (1990): 179–192.

—. *North of Empire: Essays on the Cultural Technologies of Space*. Durham, NC: Duke University Press, 2009.

Björkstén, Karin Sparring, Peter Bjerregaard, and Daniel F. Kripke. "Suicides in the Midnight Sun—A Study of Seasonality in Suicides in West Greenland." *Psychiatry Research* 133, no. 2-3 (2005): 205–2013.

Blackmore, Paul and Camille B. Kandiko. "Motivation in Academic Life: A Prestige Economy." *Research in Post-Compulsory Education* 16, no. 4 (2011): 399–411.

Bloch, Ernst. *The Principle of Hope*. Translated by Neville Plaice, Stephen Plaice, and Paul Knight. Oxford: B. Blackwell, 1986.

Bloch, Evelyn. *The Language(s) of Canadian Sport(s)*. Regina, SK: University of Regina Press, 1995.

Bonnett, John. "The Flux of Communication: Innis, Wiener, and the Perils of Positive Feedback." *Canadian Journal of Communication* 42, no. 3 (2017): 431–448.

Borden, Sally. *The Art of Economics and the Economics of Art: Making Work in Canada in the Twenty-First Century*. Montreal, QC: Black Rose Books, 2014.

Bormann, Ernest. "Symbolic Convergence Theory." In *Small Group Communication Theory & Practice: An Anthology*, 8th Edition, edited by Randy Hirokawa, Robert Cathcart, Larry Samovar, and Linda Henman, 39–47. Oxford, UK: Oxford University Press, 2003.

Bourdieu, Pierre. *Distinction: A Social Critique of the Judgment of Taste*. Translated by Richard Nice. Cambridge, MA: Harvard University Press, 1984.

Brady, Erica. *A Spiral Way: How the Phonograph Changed Ethnography*. Jackson, MS: Jackson University Press, 1999.

Braidotti, Rosi. *The Posthuman*. Malden, MA: Polity Press, 2013.

Bratton, Benjamin. *The Stack: On Software and Sovereignty*. Cambridge, MA: MIT University Press, 2016.

Braverman, Harry. *Labour and Monopoly Capitalism: The Degradation of Work in the Twentieth Century*. New York, NY: Monthly Review Press, 1998.

Brecht, Bertolt. *Brecht on Theatre*. New York, NY: Hill & Wang, 1977.

Bronnley, Cameron. "Hi, Dave: Repetition, Reversal, and Dialogism on Late-Night TV." *Cultural and Social Texts* 32, no. 3 (1991): 1204–1227.

—. "Lecture on Authenticity." University of Western Ontario, COMM 201, Fall 2007.

Bruch, Sebastian, Shuguang Han, Michael Bendersky, Marc Najork, and Mirek Plíhal. "A Stochastic Treatment of Learning to Rank Scoring Functions." *Proceedings of the 13th International Conference on Web Search and Data Mining* (2020): 61–69.

Bruner, Edward M. "Abraham Lincoln as Authentic Reproduction: A Critique of Postmodernism." *American Anthropologist* 96, no. 2 (1994): 397–415.

Burgoon, Jack and Edith Seguin. "Nonverbal Communication in the Area of Forgiveness." *Journal of Proxemics* 50, no. 2 (1993): 222–245.

Butler, Judith. *Gender Trouble: Feminism and the Subversion of Identity*. New York, NY: Routledge, 1999.

Butterfield, Paul. "Infamous and Forgotten Windsorites." *Maclean's*, Dec 24, 2001, 37.

Cameron, James (Dir.). *The Terminator*. Hemdale & Pacific Western Productions/Orion, 1984.

Cantwell, Robert. *When We Were Good: The Folk Revival*. Cambridge, MA: Harvard University Press, 1993.

Carb, Alex. *The Debates in A.I.* Chicago, IL: University of Chicago Press, 1992.

Carey, James. *Communication as Culture: Essays on Media and Society.* New York, NY: Routledge, 2008.

Cass-Beggs, Barbara, ed. *Folk Songs of Saskatchewan.* New York, NY: Folkways Records, 1963, vinyl LP.

Child, Francis James. *The English and Scottish Popular Ballads, Vols 1-10.* Boston, MA: Houghton, Mifflin & Co., 1882-1898.

Clausewitz, Carl von. *Vom Kriege.* Berlin: Dümmlers Verlag, 1832.

Coates, Ken S. *Land of the Midnight Sun.* Montreal: McGill-Queen's University Press, 2013.

Cohen, Ronald D. *Rainbow Quest: The Folk Music Revival and American Society, 1940–1970.* Amherst, MA: University of Massachusetts Press, 2002.

Cohen, Ronald D. and Rachel Clare Donaldson. *Roots of the Revival: American and British Folk Music in the 1950s.* Champaign, IL: University of Illinois Press, 2014.

Cormack, Patricia. "True Stories of Canada: Tim Hortons and the Branding of National Identity." *Cultural Sociology* 2, no. 3 (2008): 369–384.

Cornell, Daniell (Ed.). *Backyard Oasis: The Swimming Pool in Southern California Photography, 1945–1982.* Munich: PRESTEL, 2012.

Corfu, Dwight. "Hitching a Ride: Tractors, Trailers, RVs, and Large Vans in Canadian Folk Song." *Canadian Folkloristics Bulletin* 39, no. 1 (1999): 333–339.

Creighton, Helen. *Bluenose Ghosts.* Toronto, ON: Ryerson University Press, 1957.

—. *Maritime Folk Songs.* Toronto, ON: McGraw-Hill Ryerson, 1972.

—. *Helen Creighton: A Life in Folklore.* Toronto, ON: McGraw-Hill Ryerson, 1975.

Critical Art Ensemble. *The Electronic Disturbance.* Brooklyn, NY: Autonomedia, 1994.

Dean, Jodi. *Democracy and Other Neoliberal Fantasies: Communicative Capitalism and Left Politics.* Durham, NC: Duke University Press, 2009.

Dean, Michelle. "Here Comes the Hillbilly, Again: What Honey Boo Boo Really Says About American Culture." *Slate*, August 24, 2012.

Deleuze, Gilles and Félix Guattari. *Anti-Oedipus: Capitalism and Schizophrenia.* Translated by Robert Hurley, Mark Seem, and Helen R. Lane. Minneapolis, MN: University of Minnesota Press, 1983.

—. *A Thousand Plateaus: Capitalism and Schizophrenia*. Translated by Brian Massumi. Minneapolis, MN: University of Minnesota Press, 1987.

Deleuze, Gilles and Claire Parnet. *Dialogues II*. New York, NY: Columbia University Press, 2007.

Denisoff, Serge. *Great Day Coming: Folk Music and the American Left*. Baltimore, MD: Penguin Books, 1973.

Derrida, Jacques. *Of Grammatology*. Translated by Gayatri Chakravorty Spivak. Baltimore, MD: Johns Hopkins University Press, 1997.

—. *Archive Fever: A Freudian Impression*. Translated by Eric Prenowitz. Chicago, IL: University of Chicago Press, 1995.

Dewey, John. *Art as Experience*. New York, NY: Capricorn Books, 1934.

Dhariwal, Prafulla, Heewoo Jun, Christine Payne, Jong Wook Kim, Alec Radford, and Ilya Sutskever. "Jukebox: A Generative Model for Music." *arXiv preprint* arXiv:2005.00341 (2020).

Dorson, Richard. *Folklore and Fakelore*. Cambridge, MA: Harvard University Press, 1976.

Doyle, Peter. *Echo and Reverb: Fabricating Space in Popular Music Recording, 1900–1960*. Middletown, CT: Wesleyan University Press, 1997.

Duncan, William. "Anomie and Uncanniness in Digital Machinery." *Avatar* 34, no. 4 (2009): 121–129.

Dyer, Richard. *Stars*. London: British Film Institute, 1979.

—. "*A Star Is Born* and the Construction of Authenticity." In *Stardom: Industry of Desire*, edited by Christine Gledhill, 155–163. New York, NY: Routledge, 2003.

Dyer-Witheford, Nick. "Cybernetics and the Making of a Global Proletariat." *The Political Economy of Communication* 4, no. 1 (2016): 35–65.

Dyer-Witheford, Nick and Greig De Peuter. *Games of Empire: Global Capitalism and Video Games*. Minneapolis, MN: University of Minnesota Press, 2009.

Dyer-Witheford, Nick, Atle Mikkola Kjosen, and James Steinhoff. *Inhuman Power: Artificial Intelligence and the Future of Capitalism*. London: Pluto Press, 2019.

Eisenstein, Elizabeth L. *The Printing Press as an Agent of Change: Communications and Cultural Transformations in Early Modern Europe* (New York, NY: Cambridge University Press, 1979).

Eliade, Mirceau. *The Myth of the Eternal Return: Cosmos and History*. Princeton, NJ: Princeton University Press, 1905.

Engels, Friedrich. *Anti-Duhring*. Translated by Emile Burns. Moscow: Co-operative Publishing Society of Foreign Workers in the U.S.S.R., 1934.

Everett-Green, Robert. "Disc of the Week: Rebooting Canada's Folk Songbook." *Globe and Mail*, October 14, 2011.

Fabian, Johannes. *Time and the Other: How Anthropology Makes its Object*. New York, NY: Columbia University Press, 1983.

Filardo, Peter Meyer. "United States Communist History Bibliography 2018." *American Communist History* 18, no. 1-2 (2019): 97–168.

Filene, Benjamin. *Romancing the Folk: Public Memory and American Roots Music*. Chapel Hill, NC: University of North Carolina Press, 2000.

Fleet Foxes. *Fleet Foxes*. Seattle, WT: Sub Pop, 2008.

Flusser, Tina. *Ring My Bell: On the Ringing of Bells in Folk Song in Canada*. Waterloo, ON: Wilfrid Laurier University Press, 2011.

Foucault, Michel. *The Order of Things: An Archeology of the Human Sciences*. New York, NY: Pantheon, 1971.

Fowke, Edith Fulton. *Folk Songs of Canada*. Waterloo, ON: Waterloo Music Co., 1954.

—. *Folk Songs of Ontario*. New York, NY: Folkways, 1958.

—. *Lumbering Songs from the Northern Woods*. Austin, TX: University of Austin Press for the American Folklore Society, 1970.

Frazer, James George. *The Golden Bough*. London: Macmillan, 1963.

Freud, Sigmund. *Civilization and its Discontents*. New York, NY: WW Norton, 2010.

Friesen, Nicholas. "Livingston." *The Uniter*, March 19, 2014.

Frith, Simon. "'The Magic That Can Set You Free': The Ideology of Folk and the Myth of the Rock Community." *Popular Music* 1 (1981): 159–68.

Frye, Northrop. *Anatomy of Criticism: Four Essays*. Princeton, NJ: Princeton University Press, 1957.

Galli, Mark. "And God Created Football: Intimations of the Divine in a Well-Executed Screen Pass." ChristianityToday.com 28 (2010).

Galloway, Alex. *The Interface Effect*. Malden, MA: Polity, 2012.

Gamble, Fran. *Nellie the Nomad*. Waterloo, ON: Wilfrid Laurier University Press, 1991.

Garcia, David and Geert Lovink. "The ABC of Tactical Media." Post to Nettime mailing list, 1997.

Geertz, Clifford. "Deep Play: Notes on the Balinese Cockfight." *Daedalus* 101, no. 1 (1972): 1–37.

Gilday, Leela, Veronica Verkeley, and Joanna Close. *Footsteps in the Macaulay House*. Self-Published, 2007.

Gilroy, Paul. *"There Ain't No Black in the Union Jack": The Cultural Politics of Race and Nation*. London, UK: Hutchinson, 1987.

—. *The Black Atlantic: Modernity and Double Consciousness*. Cambridge, MA: Harvard University Press, 1993.

Gluck, Charles. "'Drop-Kick Me, Jesus': Religion, Faith, Language, and Ethnicity in the Canadian Football League." *The International Journal of the History of Sports* 19, no. 10 (2002): 1374–1397.

Goffman, Erving. *The Presentation of Self in Daily Life*. Norwell, MA: Anchor Books, 1959.

Goodwin, Ross. *1 The Road*. Paris: Jean Boîte Éditions, 2018.

Gramsci, Antonio. *Selections from the Prison Notebooks*. New York, NY: International Publishers, 1971.

Griffin, Sean (Ed.). *Hetero: Queering Representations of Straightness*. Albany, NY: Suny Press, 2009.

Grossberg, Lawrence. *We Gotta Get Out of This Place: Popular Conservatism and Postmodern Culture*. New York, NY: Routledge, 1992.

Guattari, Félix. *Chaosmosis: An Ethico-Aesthetic Paradigm*. Bloomington, IN: Indiana University Press, 1994.

—. *The Machinic Unconscious: Essays in Schizoanalysis*. Translated by Taylor Adkins. Los Angeles, CA: Semiotext(e), 2011.

Habermas, Jürgen. *The Structural Transformation of the Public Sphere: An Inquiry into a Category of Bourgeois Society*. Translated by Thomas Burger. Cambridge, MA: The MIT Press, 1991.

Halkman, Polk. *The Influence of Folk Tales and Ghost Stories of Newfoundland and Labrador*. Kentville, NS: Gaspereau Press, 1997.

Hall, Stuart. "Signification, Representation, Ideology: Althusser and the Post-Structuralist Debates." *Critical Studies in Media Communication* 2, no. 2 (1985): 91–114.

—. "Encoding/Decoding." In *Media and Cultural Studies: Keyworks*, edited by Meenakshi Gigi Durham and Douglas M. Kellner, 137–144. Malden, MA: Wiley-Blackwell, 2012.

Hamilton, Mary Beth. *In Search of the Blues: Black Voices, White Visions.* New York, NY: Baisc Books, 1998.

Han, Te Sun. "Folklore in Source Coding: Information-Spectrum Approach." *IEEE Transactions on Information Theory* 51, no. 2 (2005): 747–753.

Haraway, Donna. *Simians, Cyborgs, and Women: The Reinvention of Nature.* London: Free Association Books, 1996.

—. *Staying with the Trouble: Making Kin in the Chthulucene.* Durham, NC: Duke University Press, 2016.

Hardt, Michael and Antonio Negri. *Empire*. Cambridge, MA: Harvard University Press, 2001.

Hardy, Carolyn. *The Politics of Forgetting: Class, Regionalism, Gentrification, and Social Movements in Canada.* Montreal, QC: Black Thorns Press, 2012.

Harris, Sian. "The Canadian Künstlerroman: The Creative Protagonist in LM Montgomery, Alice Munro and Margaret Laurence." PhD dissertation, Newcastle University, 2009.

Harvey, David. *The Condition of Postmodernity.* New York, NY: Blackwell, 1989.

Hayhoe, Irwin. *A Heavy Time: Napoleon's Final Days.* Regina, SK: University of Regina Press, 2001.

Hayles, Katherine. *How We Became Posthuman: Virtual Bodies in Cybernetics, Literature, and Informatics.* Chicago, IL: University of Chicago Press, 1999.

Hearn, Alison. "John, A 20-year-old Boston Native with a Great Sense of Humour: On the Spectacularization of the Self and the Incorporation of Identity in the Age of Reality Television." *International Journal of Media & Cultural Politics* 2, no. 2 (2006): 131–147.

Hebdige, Dick. *Subculture: The Meaning of Style.* New York, NY: Routledge, 1979.

—. *Hiding in the Light.* New York: Routledge, 1988.

Hegel, G. W. F. *The Phenomenology of Spirit.* Translated by Peter Fuss and John Dobbins (Notre Dame, IN: University of Notre Dame Press, 2019).

Heisenberg, Werner. *The Physical Principles of Quantum Theory.* Translated by Karl Eckart and Frank C. Hoyt. Chicago, IL: University of Chicago Press, 1930.

Hempel, Birgit. *Drinking Songs of North America.* Jackson, MS: University of Mississippi Press, 1999.

Hesmondhalgh, David, and Leslie M. Meier. "Popular Music, Independence and the Concept of the Alternative in Contemporary Capitalism." In *Media Independence: Working with Freedom or Working for Free?*, edited by James Bennett and Niki Strange, 108–130. New York, NY: Routledge, 2014.

High, Rob. "The Era of Cognitive Systems: An Inside Look at IBM Watson and How It Works." *IBM Corporation Redbooks* (2012): 1–16.

Historica Canada. *Heritage Minutes: Marshall McLuhan.*

"Homer." *The Iliad.* Translated by E. V. Rieu. London, UK: Penguin, 2003.

Honour, Hazel. *Writing the World.* Toronto, ON: University of Toronto Press, 1987.

Horbinek, Raymond. *Murder and Blood in the Music and Tales of Regular People.* Calgary, AB: University of Calgary Press, 1991.

Horkheimer, Max and Theodor Adorno. *The Dialectic of Enlightenment.* Translated by Edmund Jephcott. Stanford, CA: Stanford University Press, 1972.

Innis, Harold Adams. *The Fur Trade in Canada: An Introduction to Canadian Economic History.* New Haven, CT: Yale University Press, 1930.

—. *The Cod Fisheries: A History of an International Economy.* Toronto, ON: University of Toronto Press, 1954.

—. *The Bias of Communication.* Toronto, ON: The University of Toronto Press, 1991.

—. *Empire and Communications.* Toronto, ON: Dundurn Press, 2007.

Ives, Edward D. *Folk Songs of New Brunswick.* Fredericton, NB: Goose Lane Editions, 1989.

Jameson, Frederic. *The Political Unconscious: Narrative as a Socially Symbolic Act.* New York, NY: Routledge, 2013.

Jeopardy!, "The IBM Challenge." Directed by Kevin McCarthy. February 14, 2011, ABC.

Johnston, Jesse A. "The Cimbál (Cimbalom) and Folk Music in Moravian Slovakia and Valachia." *Journal of the American Musical Instrument Society* 36 (2010): 78–117.

Jones, LeRoi. *Blues People: Negro Music in White America*. New York, NY: W. Morrow, 1963.

Kant, Emmanuel. *An Answer to the Question: What is Enlightenment?* London, UK: Penguin, 2009.

Keightley, Keir. "Reconsidering Rock." In *The Cambridge Companion to Pop and Rock*, edited by Simon Frith, William Straw, and John Street, 109–142. Cambridge, UK: Cambridge University Press, 2001.

Kelley, Robin D. G. "Notes on Deconstructing 'The Folk.'" *The American Historical Review* 97, no. 5 (1992): 1400–1408.

Kelly, Caleb. *Cracked Media: The Sound of Malfunction.* Cambridge, MA: MIT Press, 2009.

Kelly, Danny. "Here's What the NFL's New Chop Block Rule Really Means." SBNation.com, March 23, 2016.

Kennedy, Grant. *Folklore Scholarship as Folk Process*. Ottawa, ON: University of Ottawa Press, 1981.

Kierkegaard, Søren. *The Concept of Anxiety.* Translated by Reidar Thomte. Princeton, NJ: Princeton University Press, 1980.

King, Barry. "Stardom, Celebrity, and the Money Form." *The Velvet Light Trap* 65 (2010): 7–19.

Kitteringham, Marc W. "Album Review—*Artificially Intelligent Folk Songs of Canada, Vol. 1.*" *The Griff*, March, 2014.

Kittler, Friedrich. *Discourse Networks, 1800/1900*. Translated by Michael Metteer. Stanford, CA: Stanford University Press, 1990.

—. *Gramophone, Film, Typewriter.* Translated by Geoffrey Winthrop-Young and Michael Wutz. Stanford, CA: Stanford University Press, 1999.

Klane, Robert (Dir.). *Thank God It's Friday.* Los Angeles, CA: Motown Productions, 1978.

Kluitenberg, Eric (Ed.). *Book of Imaginary Media: Excavating the Dream of the Ultimate Communication Medium.* Rotterdam: NAi Publishers, 2006.

Kom, Mathias. *Artificially Intelligent Folk Songs of Canada, Vol. 2.* http://folksingularity.com/download.html.

—. "Cosmopolitan Intimacy: Antifolk in Berlin and New York." PhD dissertation, Memorial University of Newfoundland, 2017.

Kristeva, Julia. *Powers of Horror.* New York, NY: Columbia University Press, 1984.

Kucherskaya, M. A. "Wearing Folk Costumes as a Mimetic Practice in Russian Ethnographic Field Studies." *Archaeology, Ethnology & Anthropology of Eurasia* 47, no. 1 (2019): 127–136.

Kuhn, Thomas S. *The Structure of Scientific Revolutions.* Chicago, IL: University of Chicago Press, 1962.

Kurzweil, Ray. "The Evolution of Mind in the Twenty-First Century." In *Are We Spiritual Machines?*, edited by Jay W. Richards, 12–55. Seattle, WA: Discovery Institute Press, 2002.

—. *The Singularity Is Near: When Humans Transcend Biology.* New York, NY: Viking, 2005.

Lacan, Jacques. *Écrits.* Milton: Taylor & Francis, 2012.

Laney, Fran. *From Away: The Canadians Who Have Struggled South of the Border.* Montreal: McGill-Queen's University Press, 1990.

Lastra, James. *Sound Technology and the American Cinema: Perception, Representation, Modernity.* New York, NY: Columbia University Press, 2000.

Lazzarato, Maurizio. *Signs and Machines: Capitalism and the Production of Subjectivity.* Los Angeles, CA: Semiotext(e), 2014.

Ledbetter, Gabe. "Deep Sound, Deeper Spirit: Immanence in Balladry in Southwestern Ontario." *Hootenanny* 1001, no. 3 (2001): 1–30.

Lévi-Strauss, Claude. "The Structural Study of Myth." *The Journal of American Folklore* 68, no. 270 (1955): 428–444.

Levitas, Ruth. *The Concept of Utopia.* Toronto, ON: Philip Allan, 1990.

—. "Educated Hope: Ernst Bloch on Abstract and Concrete Utopia." *Utopian Studies* 1, no. 2 (1990): 13–26.

Lévy, Pierre. *Becoming Virtual: Reality in the Digital Age.* New York, NY: Basic Books, 1998.

Lidell, Geoffrey. "Information Management in the Folkloristic Context." *Song Collector Magazine* 476, no. 190 (2010): 27–28.

Lomax, Alan. *The Land Where the Blues Began.* New York, NY: Pantheon Books, 1993.

Lord, Albert Bates. *The Singer of Tales.* New York, NY: Athaneum, 1960.

Lorre, Peter. "This Year's Assumption Graduates." *Windsor Star,* June 20, 1954, A5.

Lukács, Georg. *History and Class Consciousness: Studies in Marxist Dialectics.* Translated by Rodney Livingstone. Cambridge, MA: The MIT Press, 1971.

Macpherson, James, ed. *The Poems of Ossian Translated by James Macpherson.* Translated by James Macpherson. London, UK: Strahan and T. Cadell, 1796.

Manovich, Lev. *The Language of New Media.* Cambridge, MA: The MIT Press, 2001.

Marcuse, Herbert. *An Essay on Liberation.* Boston, MA: Beacon Press, 1969.

Marshall, P. David. *Celebrity and Power: Fame in Contemporary Culture.* Minneapolis, MN: University of Minnesota Press, 2014.

Maturana, Humberto R. and Francisco J. Varela. *Autopoiesis and Cognition: The Realization of the Living Boston, MA*: D. Reidel Publishing Company, 1980.

Marx, Karl. *The Poverty of Philosophy.* Moscow: Co-operative Publishing Society of Foreign Workers in the U.S.S.R., 1935.

—. *The Economic and Philosophic Manuscripts of 1844.* Translated by Martin Milligan. New York, NY: International Publishers, 1964.

—. *The Eighteenth Brumaire of Louis Bonaparte.* New York, NY: International Publishers, 1964.

—. *Capital: A Critique of Political Economy.* Translated by Ben Fowkes. New York, NY: Vintage Books, 1977.

Marx, Karl and Friedrich Engels. *The German Ideology.* New York, NY: International Publishers, 1947.

—. *Collected Works, Volume 5.* New York, NY: International Publishers, 1976.

—. *The Communist Manifesto.* Translated by Samuel Moore. Halifax, NS: Fernwood, 1998.

Massumi, Brian. *Parables for the Virtual: Movement, Affect, Sensation.* Durham, NC: Duke University Press, 2002.

Mattern, Shannon. *Code and Clay, Data and Dirt: Five Thousand Years of Urban Media.* Minneapolis, MN: University of Minnesota Press, 2017.

Mauss, Marcel. *The Gift: The Form and Reason for Exchange in Archaic Societies.* Translated by W. D. Halls. London, UK: Routledge, 1990.

McChesney, Robert W. *Rich Media, Poor Democracy: Communication Politics in Dubious Times.* New York, NY: The New Press, 2016.

McKay, Ian. *The Quest of the Folk: Antimodernism and Cultural Selection in Twentieth-Century Nova Scotia.* Montreal, QC: McGill-Queen's University Press, 1994.

McLaughlin, Jack. "Jefferson, Poe, and Ossian." *Eighteenth-Century Studies* 26, no. 4 (1993): 627-34.

McLuhan, Marshall. *The Gutenberg Galaxy.* Toronto, ON: University of Toronto Press, 1962.

—. *Understanding Media: The Extensions of Man.* Corte Madera, CA: Ginko Press, 2003.

Mechling, Jay. "Is Hazing Play?" *Transactions at Play* 9 (2009): 45–61.

Miller, Karl Hagstrom. *Segregating Sound: Inventing Folk and Pop Music in the Age of Jim Crow.* Durham, NC: Duke University Press, 2010.

Mitchell, Gillian. *The North American Folk Revival: Nation and Identity in the United States and Canada, 1945–1980.* Burlington, VT: Ashgate Pub, 2016.

Moore, Dafydd. *Enlightenment and Romance in James Macpherson's The Poems of Ossian: Myth, Genre and Cultural Change.* New York: Routledge, 2017.

Morton, Erin. *For Folk's Sake: Art and Economy in Twentieth-Century Nova Scotia.* Montreal, QC: McGill-Queen's University Press, 2016.

Murphy, Rex and Henry Adam Svec (guest). "Does Folk song Matter Today?" *Cross-Country Checkup,* CBC Radio 1, February 2013.

Napolitano, Michael J. and Daniel H. Shain. "Four Kingdoms on Glacier Ice: Convergent Energetic Processes Boost Energy Levels as Temperatures Fall." *Proceedings of the Royal Society of London Series B: Biological Sciences* 271, no. 5 (2004): S273–S276.

Nash, Jim. "The Need for Authority in Contemporary Folkloristics." *Journal of Canadian Folklore* 120, no. 500 (2015): 259–284.

Nauright, John and Phil White. "Mediated Nostalgia, Community and Nation: The Canadian Football League in Crisis and the Demise of the Ottawa Rough Riders, 1986–1996." *Sport History Review* 33, no. 2 (2002): 121–137.

Nurse, Andrew, Gordon Ernest Smith, and Lynda Jessup, eds. *Around and About Marius Barbeau: Modelling Twentieth-Century Culture.* Gatineau, QC: Canadian Museum of Civilization, 2008.

Ong, Walter. *Orality and Literacy: The Technologizing of the Word.* New York, NY: Methuen, 1982.

Ossian, *fils de Fingal, barde du troisième siècle: Poésies Galliques traduites sur l'anglais de M. Macpherson.* 2 Vols. Paris: 1777.

Pageant, Darleen. "Local Poets Mix It Up—and Mash." *Toronto Star,* July 1967, A12.

Parikka, Jussi. *What Is Media Archeology?* Malden, MA: Polity Press, 2012.

Parry, Sharon. "Disciplinary Discourse in Doctoral Theses." *Higher Education* 36, no. 3 (1998): 273–299.

Peters, John Durham. *Speaking into the Air: A History of the Idea of Communication.* Chicago, IL: University of Chicago Press, 1999.

Peterson, Richard A. *Creating Country Music: Fabricating Authenticity.* Chicago, IL: University of Chicago Press, 2013.

Phelan, Peggy. "The Ontology of Performance." In *Performance*, edited by Philip Auslander, 320–335. New York, NY: Routledge, 2003.

Pierce, Charles Sanders. "The Sign: Icon, Index, and Symbol." In *Images: A Reader*, edited by Sunil Manghani, Jon Simons, Arthur Piper, 107–109. New York, NY: Sage Publications, 2006.

Plempton, Stan. *Once We Were Kings: My Life in Football in Canada.* Toronto, ON: Cormorant Books, 1987.

Polanyi, Karl. *The Great Transformation: The Political and Economic Origins of Our Time.* 2nd Edition. Boston, MA: Beacon Press, 2001.

Polenberg, Richard. *Hear My Sad Story: The True Tales That Inspired "Stagolee," "John Henry," and Other Traditional American Folk Songs.* Ithica, NY: Cornell University Press, 2015.

Propp, Vladimir. *Morphology of the Folk Tale*. Translated by Laurence Scott. Austin, TX: University of Austin Press, 1968.

Pugh, Vince. *The Rules of The Game: Logistics and Protocols in Canadian Football*. London, ON: Insomniac Press, 1995.

Quan-Lin, L. I. "On Taiwan Dialectical Ballads in the Period of Japanese Occupation." *Journal of Anhui University of Science and Technology* 2 (2009).

Raley, Rita. *Tactical Media*. Minneapolis, MN: University of Minnesota Press, 2009.

Rasmus, Antii, Mathias Berglund, Mikko Honkala, Harri Valpola, and Tapani Raiko. "Semi-Supervised Learning with Ladder Networks." *Advances in Neural Information Processing Systems* 28 (2015): 3546–3554.

Read, Oliver and Walter Leslie Welch. *From Tin Foil to Stereo: Evolution of the Phonograph*. Carmel, IN: HW Sams, 1959.

Richardson, Allison (Ed.). *Our Tangled Brushes, Our Tangled Limbs: An Oral History of Orgies at the Banff Centre*. Manitoba, MB: University of Manitoba Press, 2005.

Ricks, Dale. "Song Collecting Is Song Collecting." *Canadian Folkloristics Bulletin* 42, no. 1 (2004): 30–41.

—. "The Folk Songs of the Youth: Traditional Music at Upper Canada College." *Song Collecting Quarterly* 37, no. 4 (2006): 1–10.

—. "Tradition Matters: A Plea for Discernment in the Field." *Journal of Canadian Folklore* 643, no. 3 (2007): 99–101.

—. "Some Songs of Winnipeg." *Canadian Journal of Folkloristics* 103, no. 1 (2012): 51–72.

—. "Re-Centring Canadian Folk Song: Doves, Pigeons, and Other Avian Creatures." *Songbook* 14, no. 3 (2013): 220–237.

—. "Computers Cannot Make Folk Music." My Musings, Blogspot, September 15, 2015, http://mymusings.blogspot.com/2015/12/computerscannotmakefolkmusic.html.

Said, Edward. *Orientalism*. New York, NY: Pantheon Books, 1978.

Salt, Audrey. "Birds of a Feather: (Re-) Constructing Avian Images in Canadian Folk Song." *Imagination* 46, no. 43 (1999): 45–47.

Samuels, Jack F., O. Joseph Bienvenu III, Anthony Pinto, Abby J. Fryer, James T. McCracken, Scott L. Rauch, Dennis L. Murphy et al. "Hoarding in Obsessive–Compulsive Disorder: Results from the OCD Collaborative Genetics Study." *Behaviour Research and Therapy* 45, no. 4 (2007): 673–686.

Sanders, Erin. "It's Easy to Cry: The Musicality of Emotions in Portuguese, French, British, and American Balladry." *Musical Sounds* 43, no. 4 (2008): 333–380.

Sartre, Jean-Paul. *Critique of Dialectical Reason, Volume 1.* Translated by Alan Sheridan-Smith. New York, NY: Verso, 2004.

Saussure, Ferdinand de. *Course in General Linguistics.* Translated by Wade Baskin. New York, NY: Columbia University Press, 2011.

Savonius-Wroth, Celestina. "Bardic Ministers: Scotland's Gaelic-Speaking Clergy in the Ossian Controversy." *Eighteenth-Century Studies* 52, no. 2 (2019): 225-243.

Scott, Christopher. "McDiarmid Acquitted of Attempted Murder." *Yukon News*, March 5, 2015.

Searle, John. "Minds, Brains, and Programs." *Behavioral and Brain Science* 3 (1980): 417–424.

Seguin, Terry (host). *Information Morning.* CBC Radio One, 2003–Present, Fredericton.

Sennett, Richard. *The Fall of Public Man.* New York, NY: WW Norton, 1974.

Serres, Michel. *The Parasite.* Translated by Lawrence R. Schehr. Minneapolis, MN: University of Minnesota Press, 2007.

Service, Robert. *Songs of a Sourdough.* Toronto, ON: William Briggs, 1909.

Shannon, Claude Elwood. "Communication in the Presence of Noise." *Proceedings of the IRE* 37, no. 1 (1949): 10-21.

—. "The Mathematical Theory of Communication." In *The Mathematical Theory of Communication,* by Claude E. Shannon and Warren Weaver, 29–115. Urbana, IL: University of Illinois Press, 1949.

Shannon, Claude E. and Warren Weaver. *The Mathematical Theory of Communication.* Urbana, IL: University of Illinois Press, 1949.

Shelemay, Kay Kaufman. "Recording Technology and Ethnomusicological Scholarship." In *Comparative Musicology and Anthropology of Music: Essays on the History of Ethnomusicology,* edited by B. Nettl and P. Bohlman, 277–292. Chicago, IL: University of Chicago Press, 1991.

Sherif, Muzafer and Carl Hovland. *Social Judgment: Assimilation and Contrast Effects in Communication and Attitude Change*. New Haven, CT: Yale University, 1961.

Simpson, Dave. "Concert Review: A Tiresome Night for Folk Music." *London Free Press*, June 23, 1969, A7.

Skellgord, Peter. "What I Can Remember." *Globe and Mail*, Dec 26, 1992, A4.

Smith, Harry E. *Anthology of American Folk Music*. New York, NY: Folkways, 1952.

Sparks, Robert. "'Delivering the Male: Sports, Canadian Television, and the Making of TSN." *Canadian Journal of Communication* 17, no. 3 (1992): 319–342.

Spounge, Dane. *The Origins of Canadian Beat and Spoken Word Poetry*. Regina, SK: University of Regina Press, 1998.

Springer, Robert. "Folklore, Commercialism and Exploitation: Copyright in the Blues." *Popular Music* 26, no. 1 (2007): 33–45.

Sproule, Bob. "Canadian Football: Past to Present." *The Coffin Corner* 13, no. 1 (1991): 1–5.

Stallybrass, Peter and Allon White. *The Politics & Poetics of Transgression*. Ithica, NY: Cornell University Press, 1986.

Stanley, Niles J. Paul. "Vagabondage." In *The Encyclopedia of Canadian Folkloristics*, edited by Denise LaFleur, 761. Waterloo, ON: Wilfrid Laurier Press, 1985.

Storey, John. *Inventing Popular Culture*. Malden, MA: Blackwell Publishing, 2003.

Sterne, Jonathan. *The Audible Past: Cultural Origins of Sound Reproduction*. Durham, NC: Duke University Press, 2003.

Streeter, Thomas. *The Net Effect: Romanticism, Capitalism, and the Internet*. New York, NY: New York University Press, 2011.

Sturken, Marita. *Tangled Memories*. Berkeley, CA: University of California Press, 1997.

Svec, Henry Adam. "Becoming Machinic Virtuosos: *Guitar Hero*, *Rez*, and Multitudinous Aesthetics. Loading... 2, no. 2 (2008).

—. *The CFL Sessions*. Independent, 2009. http://www.thecflsessions.ca.

—. "Dissertation Proposal Defense." University of Western Ontario, September 12, 2011.

—. "On Livingston's Method." Rhubarb Festival, public lecture at Buddies in Bad Times Theatre, Toronto, 2011.

—. "'The Purpose of These Acting Exercises': The Actors' Studio and the Labours of Celebrity." *Popular Music and Society* 35, no. 3 (2011): 303–318.

—. "'Who Don't Care if the Money's No Good?': Authenticity and The Band." *Popular Music and Society* 35, no. 3 (2012): 427–445.

—. *Folk Songs of Canada Now*. Label Fantastic, 2011. http://www.folksongsofcanadanow.com.

—. *Artificially Intelligent Folk Songs of Canada*. Label Fantastic, 2013. http://folksingularity.com.

—. "Artificially Intelligent Machine Generates Authentic Canadian Folk Music." Press Release. 2013.

—. "If I Had a Hammer: An Archeology of Tactical Media." PhD dissertation, University of Western Ontario, 2014.

—. "The Songs of LIVINGSTON™." Whitewater Gallery, March 2014, North Bay, Ontario.

—. "iHootenanny: A Folk Archeology of Social Media." *The Fibreculture Journal* 25 (2015): n.p.

—. "From the Turing Test to a Wired Carnivalesque: On the Durability of LIVINGSTON's Artificially Intelligent Folk Songs of Canada." *Liminalities* 12, no. 4 (2016): n.p.

—. "L(a)ying with Marshall McLuhan: Media Theory as Hoax Art." *Imaginations* 8, no. 3 (2017) Szwed, John. *Alan Lomax: The Man Who Recorded the World*. New York, NY: Viking, 2010.

Talking Heads. "This Must Be the Place (Naive Melody)." Track #9 on *Speaking in Tongues*. Sire, 1983, LP.

Taussig, Michael. *Mimesis and Alterity: A Particular History of the Senses*. New York, NY: Routledge, 1993.

Taylor, Charles. *The Ethics of Authenticity*. Cambridge, MA: Harvard University Press, 1972.

The Invisible Committee. *The Coming Insurrection*. New York, NY: Semiotext(e), 2009.

Thibeault, Matthew D. and Julianne Evoy. "Building Your Own Musical Community: How YouTube, Miley Cyrus, and the Ukulele Can Create a New Kind of Ensemble." *General Music Today* 24, no. 3 (2011): 44–52.

Thomas, William I. and Dorothy Swaine Thomas. *The Child in America: Behavior Problems and Programs.* New York, NY: Knopf, 1928.

Thompson, Stith. *Motif-Index of Folk-Literature: A Classification of Narrative Elements in Folktales, Ballads, Myths, Fables, Mediaeval Romances, Exempla, Fabliaux, Jest-Books, and Local Legends.* Bloomington, IN: Indiana University Press, 1955–1958.

Tönnies, Ferdinand. *Community and Civil Society.* Translated by Jose Harris and Margaret Hollis (New York, NY: Cambridge University Press, 2001).

Toogood, Thomas. "Regarding the 'New Noise' in Folk Music Study." *The Blenheim News Tribune*, Dec 13, 1979, A2.

Trilling, Lionel. *Sincerity and Authenticity.* Cambridge, MA: Harvard University Press, 1971.

Trujillo, Nick. "Machines, Missiles, and Men: Images of the Male Body on ABC's Monday Night Football." *Sociology of Sport Journal* 12, no. 4 (1995): 403–423.

Turabian, Kate L. *A Manual for Writers of Research Papers, Theses, and Dissertations,* 7th Edition. Chicago, IL: University of Chicago Press, 2007.

Turing, Alan. "Computing Machinery and Intelligence." *Mind* 59, no. 236 (1950): 433–460.

University of Western Ontario Communication Studies Department. "PhD Program Expectations and Regulations." University of Western Ontario, 2008.

—. "PhD Program Graduate Student Handbook, 2008–2009." University of Western Ontario, 2008.

Vesna, Victoria. *Database Aesthetics: Art in the Age of Information Overflow.* Minneapolis, MN: University of Minnesota Press, 2007.

Virno, Paolo. *A Grammar of the Multitude: For an Analysis of Contemporary Forms of Life.* Translated by Isabella Bertoletti, James Cascaito, Andre Casson. Los Angeles, CA: Semiotext(e), 2004.

Warner, Peter. *Canadian Folk Legends and Heroes.* Winnipeg, MB: ARP Books, 2010.

Watson, John. *Marginal Man: The Dark Vision of Harold Innis.* Toronto, ON: University of Toronto Press, 2006.

Weaver, Warren. "Recent Contributions to the Mathematical Theory of Communication." In *The Mathematical Theory of Communication*, by Claude Shannon and Warren Weaver, 1–28. Urbana, IL: University of Illinois Press, 1949.

Weheliye, Alexander G. *Phonographies: Grooves in Sonic Afro-Modernity.* Durham, NC: Duke University Press, 2005.

Wheeler, Brad. "Shark Attack! Give Fans an 'Intense Musical Gyration' at New Brunswick Festival." *Globe and Mail*, July 30, 2013.

Wiebe, Rudy. *The Mad Trapper.* Markham, ON: Red Deer Press, 2003.

Wiener, Norbert. *The Human Use of Human Beings.* London, UK: Free Association Books, 1989.

Williams, Raymond. *Television: Technology and Cultural Form.* London: Routledge, 2003.

Wilmott, Glen. *McLuhan, or Modernism in Reverse.* Toronto: University of Toronto Press, 1996.

Wilson, William A. "Building Bridges: Folklore in the Academy." *Journal of Folklore Research* 33, no. 1 (1996): 7–14.

Wiseman, Fred. *A Frosty Game: The Glacial but Profound Changes in Canadian Football in the Twentieth Century.* Fredericton, NB: Goose Lane Editions, 1990.

Wood, Lynne. "Canada in the 1960s." *Local Histories* 3, no. 4 (2000): 12–17.

Yokum, Sandra. "For the Love of the Game: Exploitation in Canadian Sport." *Canadian Journal of Labour* 120, no. 3 (1993): 230–243.

Zelkovich, Chris. "Football Folk's a Passing Fancy." *Toronto Star*, August 9, 2009.

Zielinski, Siegfried. *Deep Time of the Media: Towards an Archeology of Seeing and Hearing by Technical Means.* Cambridge, MA: MIT Press, 2006.

Žižek, Slavoj. *The Sublime Object of Ideology.* New York, NY: Verso, 1989.

Zork, Bertie. "Reconsidering Nellie." *Mosaic* 22, no. 2 (1989): 230–247.

Zumwalt, Rosemary. *American Folklore Scholarship: A Dialogue of Dissent.* Bloomington, IN: Indiana University Press, 1988.

INVISIBLE PUBLISHING produces fine Canadian literature for those who enjoy such things. As an independent, not-for-profit publisher, our work includes building communities that sustain and encourage engaging, literary, and current writing.

Invisible Publishing has been in operation for over a decade. We released our first fiction titles in the spring of 2007, and our catalogue has come to include works of graphic fiction and nonfiction, pop culture biographies, experimental poetry, and prose.

We are committed to publishing diverse voices and experiences. In acknowledging historical and systemic barriers, and the limits of our existing catalogue, we strongly encourage writers from LGBTQ2SIA+ communities, Indigenous writers, and writers of colour to submit their work.

Invisible Publishing is also home to the Bibliophonic series of music books and the Throwback series of CanLit reissues.

If you'd like to know more, please get in touch: info@invisiblepublishing.com